BATTLE & BRAWL

BATTLE & BRAWL

MYTHVERSE BOOK 5

KATE KARYUS QUINN   DEMITRIA LUNETTA
MINDY MCGINNIS

CONTENTS

Visit MarleyLynn.com to sign up for the Mythverse Newsletter and you'll receive **FREE** SHORT STORIES—all set in the Mythverse!

1

―――――

The king of the gods looks down at me through Sora's eyes. A rumble of thunder booms across the stage.

"That's right, kids," Zeus says. "It seems that the news of my death was greatly exaggerated." He looks directly at Edie. "You can't get rid of me quite so easily. I'm here to take back my powers."

Reaching down, he grabs Rada's body, tearing it away from me. Then he hefts her over his shoulder, as if she were garbage.

"One down," he says. "Who's next?"

I stand, shakily, drenched in the blood of my friend. "I won the competition," I say. "I am a Queen, and you are in serious trouble."

I look to Athena to back me up. This is her school. And Rada was her student. An Amazon. Instead she's watching with an expression that can only be described as calculating, while a god with winged ankles—Hermes—whispers urgently in her ear.

No help there, I guess. Great. Having a goddess on your

side is always a positive... especially when you're facing down a god.

This is probably the point where I should quickly backpedal. Tell him I love how he's wearing Sora's face—though maybe a little blush and bronzer could help with the zombie pallor. But I can't play nice when Rada's blood is on my hands.

Instead I simply push my shoulders back, lift my chin, and repeat again, "I am the Amazon Queen."

He scoffs, such an ugly look on such a beautiful face. "Do you think that crown makes you a Queen? You are nothing. You are dirt beneath my feet. You have nothing. I am again alive, and I demand my powers back. Give me that crown now," Zeus orders in the sort of tone that silently adds, *or else I will kill you.*

Seeing as how he just killed my BRF (best roommate forever) by reaching into her midsection and tearing her nearly in two, I don't doubt his follow-through.

Zombie Sora is a real asshole.

Which is sad, because the real living Sora seemed like a pretty good guy. At least from what I could tell before he died.

I didn't know him long. He arrived here at Amazon Academy around the same time as me and eight other teenagers. We'd all been recruited to compete against each other in a series of weird tasks devised by the Greek gods. Last man—or woman, we were evenly matched —standing would become the new Zeus.

They needed a new Zeus because the old one was dead. And apparently the moment he kicked it, the whole world started crumbling to pieces. Literally. Massive earthquakes will do that. Everyone panicked and society melted away faster than the butter carving of my face Mama paid for one year at the Wisconsin State Fair. That was a damn shame, because the sculptor really captured the twinkle in my eye. And doing that with dairy products couldn't have been easy.

'Course the end of civilization was a damn shame too, although the end of the pageant circuit might have been the first thing on my mind, since that's how Mama and I made our bread and butter. Like, literally. They gave us what was left of that sculpture and we plopped it in the freezer. Ate off that thing for like three months.

So, a contest to get things back on track with a new Zeus seemed like a good idea, especially if I had a shot at being the winner. Too bad Mama didn't hang around long enough to see it pan out…she had taken one look at the Dollar Store being looted and said, "Brandee Jean, when people are fighting over Slim Jims, it's time to call it a day."

And she did, although she waited for it to be night, at least. Maybe she thought it'd be easier for me if I found her in dim lighting. Or maybe she just knew that, at her age, she looked best in the rose gold of sunset. She was positioned so that her good side was showing when I found her, so I do think some thought went into it. I popped her into the freezer next to what was left of my butter face and decided to worry about burial at a later date.

That later date hasn't come yet; competing to become the next leader of the gods has had all my attention, right up until two seconds ago when one of the supposedly dead contestants came onto the stage during my crowning and murdered my roommate - which definitely goes against his character. It does, however fit right in with what I know of Zeus. The god that's supposed to be dead, but apparently—with the assist from his brother Hades—plopped himself into Sora's body.

Which, let's be honest—good call. Sora's body was way too nice to let go to waste. Too bad the personality inside could use an attitude adjustment in the form of a sledgehammer to the head.

"Don't make me repeat myself," Zeus says. "Give me that crown, or more will die." He tosses Rada's body onto the stage floor, apparently done using it as a prop in his strutting parade.

"I heard you," I say, my hands reaching up to the crown. My fingers close around the delicate gold filigree, my thumb rubbing against the huge ruby the size of my fist. A weird rush fills me.

This is straight up old-fashioned Midwestern beauty queen anger kicking in.

Instead of removing the crown, I push it further down. Giving up a crown is just not something I can do. I won this, fair and square.

"You know, this was sized for me and it would get all bent out of shape if you tried to put it on your head. You'd look like the god of the scratch and dent sale, know what I mean?"

Zeus leans toward me and exhales angrily. His breath is so stank my eyes water. Poor Sora. He had such good hygiene. "That ruby on the crown came from the sword used to kill me. It contains my own blood. Ichor."

"Yeah, that is icky," I agree.

"Ichor!" He repeats, angrily, stomping one of Sora's feet. His big toenail splits down the center, and a maggot crawls out. Then his toe immediately heals itself. Anger fills me at the power—and the life—he took from Rada. "It's my blood! And it will never be used against me again!"

With that he grabs the crown, happy to tear my scalp right off along with it, if I don't do as he asks. Before I can even say, "Don't mess up my hair!" he flies backwards, landing on his ass.

I look behind me, wondering who came to my aid. But everyone on the stage is restrained. All the remaining contestants, my mentor, Edie, Alaric (my kind-of-guy-I-might-kiss-again-sometime-maybe and fellow contestant), as well as Lilliana—an Amazon sister and no bull-shitter who is fighting against the zombie who holds her. His forearm is shredded to the bone and he hasn't even blinked, but she's still digging away at him with her nails.

Trevor—a contestant, and Alaric's half brother—is holding Alaric back from helping me. He was part of this whole mess, helping Zeus and Hades to recover the crown.

Artemis and Athena are oddly still, along with all the other gods there to perform the ceremony. Hermes still stands beside Athena, a hand on her arm now. None of them are interfering, only watching intently as the drama plays out onstage. Why aren't they helping? The audience, comprised mostly of Amazons—and all of them armed to the teeth—have been efficiently flanked by an army of the undead streaming down the aisles.

We're pretty evenly matched, number-wise. But if this goes wrong—and it's looking like it will—Amazon blades don't stand a chance against bodies that don't die. I've got to walk this back, and fast.

"What the Hades?" Zeus sits up, clearly rattled by the blow that someone dealt him when he tried to take my crown. "Who hit me?"

Suddenly, I feel it. Mother Hippolyta. The spirit of the Amazons. She entered me during the final contest, like a sort of blessing. She recognized me as a true Amazon, which means I've got to protect my sisters-in-arms.

Or fight and die with them.

And, let's be honest, by the look of the zombies around here, I'm not in a big hurry to rot and die. Especially if that means Hades gets to tell my dead body what to do. I mean…ew.

"Stop!" I cry out, just as Zeus is coming back to his feet.

Hippolyta's strength rolls through my voice, and he obeys as if he were a dog. It only lasts a second, but it's enough. Athena's head snaps in my direction, the voice of Hippolyta spurring her to action. She stomps down on one of Hermes' ankle wings, and it breaks like a baby bird hitting an eighteen-wheeler at sixty-five miles an hour. The god howls in pain as Athena easily sidesteps around him.

"The contest has finished, Father." Athena declares. "We have a new Queen."

Artemis steps beside her. "You cannot come here, kill our Amazons." Her voice actually catches when she looks at Rada. "You died."

"You should have stayed dead!" I add, but no one looks at me.

"My brother, Zeus, stands here before us. Alive. Athena, you called him Father, so clearly you recognize him despite the change in form!" Hades exclaims, his voice bellowing throughout the amphitheater. "It's a dangerous precedent, giving away a god's powers. If Athena lets this mortal girl from Milktown, USA have Zeus' powers, whose powers will she strip next?" Hades addresses this to the gathered gods. A low murmur sweeps through them and a few heads even nod in agreement.

"Absurd," Athena says, but even she doesn't sound as certain.

"I declare this entire contest moot!" Hades says, taking charge. "All in agreement, say aye."

2

———

"Wait, what?!" I clamp my hands tighter on my crown, Hippolyta's strength having deserted me. These are regular old human fingers holding onto this crown, without the strength of Zeus, but I know I've got a good grip. There's a reason I won the All Midwest Milkmaid Competition three years running.

"You do not call a vote on my campus!" Athena thunders at Hades.

"Moot!" Hades repeats, raising his arms for silence as Zeus climbs to his feet, Sora's bruised and battered body healing before our eyes.

"Brandee Jean has won, uncle," Athena says, clenching her jaw.

"This contest was begun on the assumption that Zeus had died, and we needed a new king of the gods," Hades goes on, but is interrupted.

"He was dead!" Edie, my shifter-mentor cries out, breaking free from the zombie who held her. "I killed him!"

"Um, yeah..." Jordan, one of the contestants' mentors, adds.

Hepa, who was Rada's mentor, steps forward as well. "Edie killed you, then she burned your body."

"Why are all my children so ungrateful?" He turns to Edie. "You did burn my body, didn't you?" Zeus asks Edie, cocking his head to the side and smiling with Sora's mouth in a way that can still make me melt a little. "So I found a new one," Zeus finishes.

"And now," Hades says, "he's no longer dead."

"Hail!" Zeus cries. "Long live Zeus!" He begins a chant, which he's clearly expecting his entourage to pick up. But Trevor is too busy whispering shit-talk into Alaric's ear and Hermes is still moaning over his broken ankle wing. Hades encourages his zombie army to give Zeus a round of applause, but when they comply a few rotted hands come flying off the end of their arms instead.

"You may be back, but your powers did not return to you automatically," Athena says, quickly drowning out the half-assed support. "You are no more king of the gods than this idiot is," she says, motioning to Hermes.

"What?" Hermes asks. His ankle wing has finally healed and he's shaking out his leg. "Did I miss something?"

"I put forth that BJ is now the sole owner of your powers.," Athena corrects. "We will complete the ceremony as planned."

"I second," Artemis says and a few gods mutter their agreement. But many glance towards Hades and remain silent, clearly still remembering his words.

"Well, I put forth that gods are gods and girls are girls, and that's the way it should stay! All powers should be returned to Zeus, the rightful king of the gods," Hades says. "So there!"

Athena glances at her fellow gods, gathered on the stage. I can see her weighing the potential outcome if she held a vote right now.

"This isn't right," Alaric shouts, finally breaking free of Trevor with a satisfying punch. He comes to my side. Zahara —a harpy with super smarts—flutters over as well. Her manticore mentor follows. Trevor glares at us. The other contestants don't seem to know what to do. Sophia—a vampire princess—and her mentor Tina are strangely quiet, waiting for things to play out.

"We need time to discuss," Athena says finally. "The gods will vote."

"Oh hell no," I say, shrugging off Alaric's arm as he tries to stop me from advancing on Athena. "I won this crown!"

"Do you doubt the sovereignty of the gods?" Artemis thunders.

"If that means do I think that none of you have any business telling anyone else what to do, then yeah, I very much doubt your sover-inity."

Artemis intercepts me easily, leading me to the side of the stage. "We're trying to save your skinny ass!" she hisses into my ear.

"Excuse me, don't comment on the amount of junk in my trunk. It's been a stressful few weeks. I haven't gotten my squats in," I snap, but I'm already offstage, the bickering of the gods and the murmur of the audience reduced to a low murmur. Hades calls off his zombies and Athena announces to the Amazons that there is a truce until further notice.

"We'll probably have a redo," Alaric says as he falls into step beside me. "It's the only thing that makes sense."

"I'm not doing this all over again," I moan, sinking onto a step, my head in my hands. "I can't."

"You can, Brandee Jean. And you will," a voice above me says.

I look up and if I weren't already sitting I would have fallen down. It can't be.

She ignores him, her eyes on me. "You get back up on

those spike heels and take this one in the teeth. It's round two, baby girl, and Mama's in your corner now."

3

"Mama?" I ask. She's in front of me, larger than life. I reach out a hand but can't make myself touch her. She's pale and freezer burnt; some of her skin is worn away to reveal pink muscle at her collarbone and elbows. She's dressed in her favorite dress, the one that's cut a little low with the skirt that's a little high. She always loved to show off her assets.

"It's me, Brandee Jean."

I shoot to my feet, fury blasting through every bit of my body. Where is that absolute dickhead, Hades? Why did he do this? Just to mess with me?

"Baby," Mama's hand rests on my arm. "Aren't you happy to see me?"

Tears well up in my eyes then. Rada's murder. Sora's body getting taken by Zeus. And now Mama here in front of me.

It's all a lot to handle.

Even though Mama was never the cuddly hugging type, I can't stop myself from throwing my arms around her and squeezing tight, which, I quickly realize I've got to be careful about because while Mama always was proud of her squishy bits, it seems all of her bits are squishy now.

"Mama! I missed you so—"

"Brandee Jean!" Mama peels me off and pushes me back so hard that I would've fallen on my ass if Alaric didn't catch me. "Get yourself under control. First off, you know how I feel about crying."

"Nobody looks good with puffy eyes," I automatically reply.

"That's right." Mama nods. "Secondly, where was your head when you put me in that freezer? Sure, I'm happy not having dirt under my fingernails. But you knew power was iffy. I defrosted and re-froze so many times, I had to coat my whole self with hairspray after waking up just to get everything tight." She shakes her head at me and I know this expression well. It's the disappointed one. I did good, but not quite good enough. "You shoulda hooked that freezer up to a generator. One with a good supply of fuel to keep it going. Maybe then I'd be able to handle a hug without worrying over whether I'll fall to pieces."

I gulp. Chastened and look down at my feet. "I'm sorry, Mama."

Her hand cups my chin, making me meet her eyes. "I did miss you, baby girl." Her other hand goes to the crown on my head, softly running her fingers over it. "And I'm real proud of this crown you got yourself here. You did real good."

We're suddenly interrupted by Artemis' booming voice making an announcement. "Under terms of our truce all Amazons and zombies must leave the auditorium. Contestants and mentors stay here. Gods will confer in Athena's temple."

The zombies begin shuffling out, Amazons alongside them, none too happy. A few zombies are leaving with fewer limbs, truce or not. My mama releases me and takes a step back.

"Wait!" I call.

"I can't, baby. I'm just another zombie in Hades' army. He agreed to these terms, so i've got to go where he says.," she explains. "But I won't leave you again, not this time. I promise."

She's under Hades' control. She can't make that promise.

"I'll find you as soon as this is all sorted," she tells me.

Still up on stage, Sora—no, he's no longer Sora, he's Zeus—is making a scene. Shaken from my mama literally coming back from the dead I barely pay attention.

"I am a god!" Zeus is shouting. "I should get voting rights."

"You are a contestant." Athena booms. "You stole Sora's body. You will stay here while your fate is determined!"

"I will represent you, brother," Hades assures him, giving a double thumbs up on his way out.

Athena is the last god to leave. For the first time sorrow appears on her face as she approaches Rada's body. She picks up Rada's remains as if she weighs nothing at all.

"My fine Amazon," she says. "You will be joining the honored dead." Cradling Rada as one would a baby, she walks away and disappears.

"Wait!" I yell at the spot where Athena just stood. "Don't we get to say goodbye? Or attend the funeral?"

Edie's arm comes around my shoulder. "I'll do what I can to allow you to be part of the burial ceremony. You deserve that."

Zeus stands, his eyes narrowing as they take in Edie and me together. "The two of you are in cahoots, then?"

In an instant Edie shifts into her dragon self. Smoke watts from her nostrils as she glares down at Zeus. With the twitch of a wing, she pushes me behind her. I probably should push myself forward again. Insist on taking Zeus on together. But I'm tired and Edie looks like she's got this.

Sophia flexes her back and then flies up into the air. "If we're gonna have an unofficial rumble to figure this all out, then I'm throwing my hat back into the ring."

"Me too," Malik quickly echoes, shifting into his lion form.

Zahara sighs. "BJ isn't the one fighting. It's her mentor and Zeus...who obviously are working out some daddy-daughter issues."

"Ew, no," Edie quickly says.

"Ungrateful child," Zeus counters. "You were happy enough to call me father when you wielded the blade that would kill me."

"My goodness," Trevor tsks softly. "It must be awkward around the table during the holidays."

There's something about the image of Edie in her dragon form sitting at opposite ends of a big holiday table from Zeus that makes me snort with laughter.

"Now, if it's anything like my family," Trevor continues, "everything will be completely civil on the surface. One does not make a scene when the two-hundred-year-old crystal is on the table. But every request, even the most banal, like 'please pass the salt,' will be understood by all to mean, 'I hate you and will one day piss on your grave.'"

I glance at Trevor, realizing that he's purposely trying to release some of the tension here. If he wasn't a totally despicable person, I'd suspect he was trying to prevent more bloodshed. But Trevor doesn't do anything that won't benefit himself in some way, so there must be another angle he's working.

Before I can figure it out, Zahara chips in. "Harpies believe that no celebration is complete without bloodshed."

"My family likes only our meal to be bloody," Malik adds,

shifting back to human. "But one year, my Dad tried to convince my mom he should have multiple wives like a real lion." Laughing, Malik shakes his head. "Oh man, that did not work out for him."

Zeus' eyes dart between us, suspicious. "Why is everyone laughing? I thought we were all going to murder one another?"

Sophia's mentor, Tina, laughs. "I'm a vampire and even I think you need to maybe be a little less bloodthirsty."

Sophia settles on the ground beside her mentor. As a stuck-up vampire princess, Sophia thinks everyone is below her. Even her mentor. She takes a moment to send some stink-eye Tina's way before adding, "I don't think it's blood he wants. It's power. I don't understand why the gods would just leave him here with us."

"The gods have not left you unprotected. They put up a shield," someone says. It's Trevor's mentor, the one dating—if dating is the word—Zahara. Colin, the fae. "None of you can touch each other until they return."

We absorb that for a moment. Then, with a snarl, Zeus launches himself at Sophia. She gasps as he freezes only inches away from her. Tina's fangs flash, but there's no need for defense. The fae was right. Zeus, after remaining frozen for several long seconds, suddenly goes limp and falls to the ground.

We all stare at him. Then, with a sigh, Trevor goes over and kneels beside Zeus, encouraging him to sit up and shake it off.

I turn away, not wanting to see anymore. Alaric stands to leave.

"Don't go… I don't want to be alone, I just…I don't want to hear how it's all gonna be okay."

Alaric sits again. "You want to hear how it's *not* going to be okay?"

"No!" I put my face in my hands. "I just want to not think about Zeus at all. Can we just rewind to before he showed up? Actually, let's rewind all the way back to when Sora was still alive and Trevor wasn't a total dick—"

"Trevor was always a total dick," Alaric interrupts.

"True. But I didn't know it yet." I peek up at Alaric from beneath my eyelashes. "I also still thought that you were an uptight stuffed shirt."

"I am those things," Alaric corrects again, although this time with a twinkle in his eye. "You just realized those are my good qualities."

I laugh despite myself. It feels good to find humor in something even when everything is so bleak.

"See, this is why you need a mentor. They might've advised you to not immediately play the snooty aristocrat card."

"Yeah, well, I didn't realize the mentors were so important. When we were told about the competition Colin actually came with another fae. My father was beside himself. Imagine spending generations trying to get the magic out of your bloodline and suddenly two full blooded faeries are standing in your drawing room, telling you your children need to compete to be a god." He lets out a hollow laugh.

"Father wanted us to take part...I mean that's a lot of power on the line. But he didn't want us to be linked with the fae. Trevor and I agreed that we would decline our mentors. I did."

"And he didn't..." I finish.

Alaric shrugs. "That's my brother."

I glare at where Trevor and Zeus stand across the auditorium. I wish I could lay hands on them. I'd crush them to a pulp. Zeus catches my eye.

"Hey, pretty princess. Hades brought your mom back for you," he says.

I glare at him and say nothing. I'm still processing the whole Momzbie thing and don't really want to discuss it with Zeus.

But he's not gonna let it go. "If you forfeit the crown now, before the gods make their decision, just say that I'm the winner, I'll have him bring Rada back too."

No. They couldn't. Could they?

I can't help but imagine Rada back in our dorm room. Her bed across from mine. Really, we were just starting to become friends. She was strong and certain and determined. And also one of those girls who didn't care for anything frivolous. And she thought I was the most frivolous thing on the entire planet. Until the end. When she called me her Amazon sister and declared the crown should go to me.

Bringing her back...isn't that what a sister would do?

"BJ, I know it's tempting." Edie's hand lands on my back. "But you can't trust Zeus."

"Hades has been raising the dead left and right. You've all seen the zombies. What's not to trust?" Zeus assures me from Sora's beautiful face.

I look at Edie. "I know you want me to win, but Rada…"

"Rada would not want to be a zombie," Hepa says, her voice firm. "She died an Amazon. She was a warrior. She would not want to be trapped in a chunk of rotting flesh, a pale imitation of what she used to be." Hepa is right. Rada would hate being a zombie. She would have seen being brought back like that as a betrayal.

"I take offense…" Zeus begins but I don't let him finish.

My hands ball into fists as I advance on Zeus. "Screw you, you friend killing, body snatching, world destroying bastard. You can have this crown when you pry it from my cold dead hands."

He smiles in this lazy way that doesn't reach his dead eyes. "That sounds just fine, missy."

I'm about to see how strong Athena's word against us touching each other really is when she appears.

"A decision has been reached," she tells us. "One which nobody likes, but to which we've all agreed." Athena turns to me and gives a slight shake of her head that tells me the vote didn't go my way. And then she confirms it. "We have decided the last contest was indeed moot, due to Hades interference."

Edie sighs heavily and her shoulders sink, but nobody protests or says it's unfair.

Funny, when I was getting crowned it felt like everyone was behind me. Well, maybe not Sophia, but she wasn't actively booing or anything. Sure, everything went sideways in that last contest, what with the zombies taking the field, but Rada and I were the last two standing. And she stepped down. Purposely. She wanted me to take the crown.

And now it's all being undone, and no one's gonna say a word.

Not even Alaric. His face is carefully neutral as Athena continues.

"We have designed a final test, which will include all current contestants and" —she clears her throat— "Zeus."

"Yes!" Zeus punches the air. "In your faces!"

Trevor sighs and mutters, "Show some chill, man."

Alaric laughs, low and cold. "Indeed. Were Father to see your so-called god, he would certainly have to rethink his belief in the natural superiority of old blood."

"Yeah, Zeus is a classless ass. Now can we find out what the next test is?" Edie cuts in.

"You will all be brought to an island and stripped of your powers."

"Survivor?" Malik says. "We got this, bro!" he tells Jordan.

"Only contestants," Athena clarifies. "No mentors."

Edie bristles. "But anything could happen."

"That's the point," Zahara says.

"Are we meant to kill each other?" Trevor asks, seeming open to the possibility.

"No." Athena looks like one more snide comment will put her over the edge. The lady is clearly not used to people talking back. "Similar to capture the flag, you will each attempt to take something from the other contestants. A special item. The goal is to collect all the items and figure out the puzzle. The first person to do so will be crowned King—or Queen—of the gods."

"But we *can* kill each other, right?" Zeus asks. "There's no rule against it?"

"Dude, aren't you already dead?" Malik asks.

"And without Rada's healing powers…" Zahara says.

"Ew. Gross," Sophia wrinkles her nose.

"You're gonna get real rank, real fast," I say, trying to get back into the spirit of competition with a little shit-talking.

The truth is, though, that I'm tired. And I want this to be over. I thought it was done. And now we're just starting it all up again.

"Mentors, you have five minutes with your mentees." Everyone else pairs up with their mentors, Sophia with Tina, Zahara with her manticore, and Edie with me. Colin, instead of speaking to Trevor, goes to Alaric, while Trevor and Zeus huddle together and look unhappy.

"Brandee, you have got this," Edie tells me, but she sounds more desperate than certain.

"I do?"

"Look, you won't have your physical strength, but you are strong where it counts. Zeus will try to get in your head. He'll play as dirty as they come. But don't just watch out for him and Trevor. They all want to win. Even Alaric. Even

Zahara. They are not your friends. They are your competition."

"Rada was my friend." I feel a wave of grief ready to wash me away. "She should have won."

Edie shakes her head. "Rada was amazing, but so are you. You are a fighter. You are a winner. You are an Amazon."

She wraps me in a hug; even her wings sweep around my body.

Athena's voice booms through the auditorium. "Time is up."

The lights go out and for a moment I think I've passed out but the next moment I'm standing on sand, looking out at a beautiful beach and the blue of the ocean.

My heels sink. I sigh.

"Here we go again," I say to the endless ocean.

4

I bring my hands up to my head.

My crown is still there.

The feel of it beneath my fingertips is all that keeps me from sinking into the sand and crying my little eyes out.

Athena said the contest was moot. That we're having a complete do-over. But she let me keep the crown. Is that her way of saying she's rooting for me? Or does it just mean that she was afraid of crossing Hippolyta? Or did the gods just half-ass this whole thing?

Either way, it's a timely reminder. I won this once. I can do it again.

I am Brandee Jean. Maybe not yet the Amazon Queen, but at least a princess.

And anyway, having grown up with pageants, I know what it is to have a crown and then have to fight for it again.

One year, this cheese-of-the-month club had a pageant every month to celebrate their mailing. I got the crown in January (gouda), lost it in February to Missy Hinkle, won it again in March (cheddar), and then held on to it through the next four months until in August I was brought down by the overwhelming stink of limburger. After wearing that crown for so long, it had started to feel like my own. But on the pageant circuit, you gotta constantly earn the right to wear the crown.

Now, I gotta figure out how to hold onto this one.

Time to take stock of the situation.

Okay, my feet are sinking faster than my hair is frizzing up in this humidity. I've always been a land-locked girl, but even I can see this water is rising fast. Since I never did learn to swim—Mama always said suits are made for walking, not getting wet—I need to find higher, drier land. That's easy enough. I point myself toward a dune and pull my feet out of the muck—it's past my ankles now—and get onto the hill, where I flop forward.

It's not exhaustion. Not physical, anyway. It's purely emotional. I won the ultimate prize, had it taken away from me, watched my friend die, and then got Mama back…kind of. There's still a whiff of her about me from that hug. I can tell she was next to some pork in that freezer, and she wasn't kidding about the defrosting and refreezing doing a number, on her and the pork both.

I imagine her sitting up in that freezer, realizing she was dead, and had to answer to Hades, and then heading straight to the bathroom to see what we had in there that might help freshen up a corpse. That's Mama for you, always taking inventory of her battle chest. I mean that literally; the women in our family have always been blessed with the sort of assets that don't need padded bras. But Mama had some good ideas, and she could always sum up a situation, which is what I should be doing now.

Maybe I should ask myself what Momzbie would do. And she would figure out what she had on her that she could use to her benefit. "Usually two things, if you get my meaning," she'd say, hefting her bra.

First off, I definitely have my boobs. Check.

What else?

Luckily, the gods were kind enough to trick me out in some sort of Lara Croft gear. At least I'm not wearing that ball gown I had on for the crowning ceremony. I mean, it was super glam, but I'm already sweating through these chinos and that does not make the sand in my ass situation any better. I'm going to have to dig around in there, which is not ideal when I'm fresh out of hand sanitizer.

The tide is licking at my feet—again? Surely this is not right. I move further inland, finding some shade under a sparse copse of trees. I run my hands through my pockets, checking first to see if I've got anything to eat. Nope, nada on the food situation. Which, as a beauty contestant, isn't that big of a concern for me. "Fast or you'll have a huge ass," was one of Mama's bumper stickers. Luckily, my survival gear does include water, which I'm a little surprised by. The gods tend to forget that we humans have needs. The canteen slaps against my leg as I search my pockets.

Yes, humans have needs. Like…keys.

"What the frick?" I ask the sky, as I pull a long, delicate silver key from my side pocket.

I hold the key up to the sun, where it reflects so brightly I bring it back down, fast. Nothing like signaling to the enemy where I am.

What did Athena say? We were each given a piece of a puzzle, and we're supposed to try to steal each other's piece, then solve it.

Or just kill each other. That was Zeus' version.

I cannot forget that wherever this place is, he's here, too. Zeus, running around inside of Sora's body. Alaric, Trevor, Sophia, Zahara and Malik are here, too. The water licks at me again, and I'm moving, suddenly aware of the danger— and not just of the water. I'm not alone here, and if the water is pushing me further inland, that means it's pushing everyone else, too. They're going to force us to cross paths, and then…

I remember the sound of Rada's body hitting the stage as Zeus tossed her aside. I slip the key back into my pocket, then realize that's too easy for anyone trying to grab it off me. I study the key for a moment. It almost looks like a comb. A busted one, but I still think it will work.

Removing the crown, I carefully shove it down the front of my shirt, not wanting it on the ground. Then I tease the hair on the top of my head with the jagged edge of the key. I'm going for a sorta messy castaway chic look. I've got a good thick head of hair so it takes some time to work through the whole top of my head. Finally, though, it's a nice little nest for me to nestle the key against my scalp, artfully arrange my hair over it, and then secure the whole thing with the crown.

I use the side of my silver canteen as a rough mirror and take a moment to admire my handiwork.

I like this look.

Big hair. Big attitude.

It says Brandee Jean is here to win this thing.

"I'm coming for your ass, Zeus," I say.

I'm still holding the canteen in my hands. It's nice and solid. Thick. I can imagine myself slamming it into Zeus' face and smashing his nose flat.

I've never been the bloodthirsty 'anything to win' type of person.

Going after Zeus isn't about winning. It's about Rada.

The way he tore her open and then tossed her aside. The moment burns like acid in my gut.

Water laps at my toes once more.

Damn.

Focus up, Brandee Jean. The time will come to go mano a

mano with Zeus, but until then I need to get through this challenge.

Which means holding onto my key. And getting everyone else's puzzle piece. And solving the puzzle.

Well, at least I know that keys open things.

I've just got to figure out what. And also not die.

———

I find a small stream and refill my canteen; running from the oncoming tide is thirsty work. Keeping my head up, I'm on high alert the entire time.

There's a shuffling in the trees to my left, and I dodge behind a rock, dumping cold stream water all over my leg as I do. I hunker down, peering over the edge of the boulder, trying to locate the sound of the shuffling.

There, a flutter of movement catches my eye, and I spot Zahara up in the tree. We were all stripped of our powers, which means we've been returned to our normal state. Which means I'm still dead sexy, which is great, but it also means that I'm just a human. Zahara is a harpy, and she took advantage of that, fast. She's perched in the tree, wings closed tightly around her as she scans the horizon.

And if Zahara still has wings, then it's good to remember that Sophia will still have her vampire teeth as well, and Malik will be able to shift into a lion. The gods might have stripped us of our powers that we inherited from Zeus, but that still leaves the humans with the short end of the stick. Technically, Trevor and Alaric are fae, but neither one of them have ever seemed anything more than human to me.

Unless maybe Alaric sometimes shrinks to the size of a pixie and puts on a little green dress for kicks.

I laugh aloud. I can't help it. I was built for the spotlight, not to hide in the shadows.

Zahara spots me at once, and dive bombs from her perch. She's got me flat on my back in no time, and I'm scrambling, scratching at her arms, kicking, even trying out a little tae kwon do from the two week class I took one time when Mama decided that should be my new talent. I wasn't good at it then. I'm not good at it now. Plus, I'm on my back like a turtle and that is not the best way to start a scuffle.

Zahara plants her hand over my mouth and I'm about to bite down on it when her wide eyes meet mine. She's got one finger to her lips, shushing me. And it's not anger in her eyes; it's fear. Zahara isn't trying to kill me, she's trying to warn me.

I nod that I understand, and sit up. We're both crouching behind the rock when Sophia comes into view. She's got on the same outfit as Zahara and I—apparently the gods are short-shrifting this contest—and her pale skin is already a harsh shade of red, raised blisters forming alongside her jawline.

Shit. While being a vampire has the advantage of built-in razor teeth, it also has the disadvantage of being fried by the sun. We're on a desert island, and Sophia's skin is not standing up to the rays. She staggers, shuddering into the cool water to splash around, then drags herself into the shade.

Zahara and I look at each other, silently asking each other the same question.

We arrive at the answer together, and step out from behind the rock to help Sophia.

"Pssstt…" Zahara whispers, and Sophia rolls, pulling a knife from a sheath on her ankle.

Zahara puts her arms up, and I follow along behind, trying to look friendly. Which is pretty easy when all you've got on you for a weapon is a canteen and you're facing down a vampire with a Bowie knife.

Well, a crispy vampire. Damn… Sophia does not look good.

"We're not going to hurt you," Zahara says, coming to the vampire's side. She helps her further into the shade, and I hand her my canteen. Instead of drinking, she dumps it over her head, causing an audible sizzle. Steam rises up from her hair.

"They didn't give you sunscreen?" I ask, and Sophia shakes her head.

"I don't have water," Zahara says.

"I wasn't given food," I chip in. "But wait, Sophia got a knife?"

Sophia leans back against a tree. "No. Found it," she says, breathlessly. "There are weapons, if you keep your eyes open."

"Weapons," Zahara says, brow furrowing. "I suppose a knife could be helpful for hunting and gathering."

"Yeah, or just simply hunting," Sophia sneers. And then to make sure we got it, "Like each other."

Zahara rolls her eyes. "Yes, thank you for clarifying. I can still connect the dots without Zeus' god-like wisdom." She sighs. "Though I will admit, it would've come in handy with the whole puzzle thing."

"Well, I don't miss flying," Sophia says. "Without sunscreen I have no interest in getting closer to the sun."

"If I had my super strength still," I chime in, "I could pull down some trees and make you shelter."

Sophia shoots me a poisonous look. "Or you could crush me to death with your bare hands."

Zahara and I exchange a glance, and I remember how I'd felt when she dive-bombed me from the tree. I'd definitely thought she was going to kill me. And that was Zahara, someone I'd call a friend under different circumstances. I take a few steps back from Sophia, just out of striking distance. She notices, and laughs.

"Don't worry, I don't have it in me," she says. "Not that I wouldn't love to kill you. I just can't."

"Nice. Friends?" I ask, and she actually smiles, which might be sweet, except one of her blisters breaks on her jaw when she does.

"Not quite," she says, pulling her key from her pocket. Sophia's is made of jade, a soft glow emanating from it as she turns it in her hands.

"No, we're not friends," she says. "But it's pretty obvious I won't be winning this thing. So here's what I want, before I turn into a pile of ash."

She holds the key in front of her, eyes darkly fixated.

"I want to see you two fight each other for it."

5

———

Zahara and I eye each other and I catch her slight smile. I laugh.

"We're not gonna fight," I tell Sophia.

"Not over your key, you evil bitch," Zahara adds. "We'll be able to take it from your corpse soon enough."

"Well, you can't both have it," Sophia says through dry cracked lips.

"How are you not..." I pause.

"Already ash," Zahara finishes for me.

Sophia barks out a laugh. "I applied my sunscreen yesterday. It will become less and less effective."

"Maybe we can..." I look around. Crap, the tide is still approaching. "Look, if I help you, do you promise not to bite me?" I ask.

"Would you believe me anyway?"

"No," Zahara says at the same time I say, "Yes."

"Look, Brandee," Zahara tells me. "I'm not helping this blood sucker. I'm going to have a look around the island. If you want to help her...you can have her key after she..."

"Dies," Sophia finishes. "Although I technically am already

dead."

"Maybe we'll have to fight if it's only you and me left," Zahara says with a shrug. "Don't worry, though. I'll try not to scratch up your pretty face, okay?"

"No, Zahara, that's not okay."

She frowns. "BJ, it's a fight. I'll do my best not to leave scars where it will show, but I've got talons, so there's only so much I can do."

"No! That's not what I mean!" The words explode out of me. I can't believe Zahara is talking so casually about us fighting it out. "I don't want to fight you at all. I thought we were friends. And I..." I can't say 'I won,' it sounds too pathetic. But my hand goes up to my crown, giving my intention away.

"Pwease don't take my pwetty cwown," Sophia mocks in a stupid baby voice.

Zahara's eyes soften. She takes my arm and pulls me away from Sophia. Leaning in she says in a soft voice, "I'm sorry. I know you won and I know Rada wanted you to have the crown. But..." She hesitates. "I didn't see a leader on that stage today. Yeah, Zeus showing up was shocking, but even after, you seemed stunned. You couldn't handle it. The leader of the gods can't check out when things get tough."

I don't say anything. I don't know what to say. Everything was crazy and it's true I was overwhelmed. But Zahara makes it sound like I totally choked. Did I?

"Look, I hope it doesn't come down to you and me," Zahara says.

I swallow back the bitterness rising in my throat. "You mean that you hope someone else takes me out so you don't have to."

She gives me a sad smile that tells me I nailed it. "If it helps, you can keep the crown if I win. It's not really my style."

Once again my hand goes to the crown. For the first time in my life, though, a sparkly tiara doesn't feel like enough. In fact, it feels like a pretty lousy consolation prize.

Zahara gives me a final pat on the back. "Good luck. I'm gonna go take out the truly bad people," she says as she jumps into the air. "Keep an eye out for the others!"

I watch as she becomes a speck in the sky and then disappears behind some treetops.

I don't know what's worse. That Zahara is so willing to fight me. Or that she's so certain she would win.

Either way, it's put a serious dent in my confidence.

I turn to find Sophia staring at me with a knowing smirk. "So...what are you going to do, BJ Queen?"

I straighten my crown. "I'm going to get you to some shade. If you bite me and turn me into one of you, I'm going to whittle a wooden stake and put it right through your icy heart." I lean down and help her up.

"Just because you're bitten by a vampire doesn't mean you become a vampire, you ignorant human," she tells me as I haul her along.

She's heavier than she looks and I wish I had my strength back. "Almost there," I grunt.

"You're an idiot for helping me," Sophia says. "I never liked you."

"The feeling is absolutely mutual," I say as I dump her in some shade. "If you're out of the sun, you'll be fine, right?"

She nods then begrudgingly adds, "Thank you."

"I'm going to go look around, but I'll come back to check on you…"

"BEEEEEEEEJAAAAAAAY," someone yells in the distance. "Come out and plaaaaaay."

"Zeus," Sophia hisses. I bend down to help her up. "No," she pushes me away.

"We have to go, like now," I tell her. The catcalling is

closer, his voice rising up and down in a maniacal sing-song.

"LITTLE LION, LITTLE FAE, COME OUT AND PLAY!" Zeus yells.

"Sophia, come on," I whisper, but she goes limp.

"Go. Hide," Sophia tells me. "I'm not surviving this. I'm gonna do as much damage to that bastard as I can before I go out, though."

"We can hide you," I tell her. "Ride it out until the end. You can live."

She flashes her teeth at me. "Are all humans as ignorant as you are?" She thrusts her key at me. "I'd rather you had it than Zeus."

I clutch it to my chest.

"Go, or I *will* bite you," she tells me.

I barely have time to duck behind some trees before Zeus makes an appearance, Trevor trailing behind. Zeus swings two keys…

My heart skips a beat at the sight of that second key. Alaric! My brain shouts. Trevor would encourage Zeus to go after him first. Alaric is big and strong, but Zeus would fight dirty and Alaric probably would see that as beneath his honor or some crap like that. I can see it now, Zeus throwing sand in Alaric's eyes on the beach, dragging him to the ever-rising surf, shoving his head under…

I am spiraling downward when the logical part of my brain reasserts itself.

Trevor had a key too. And he would immediately give his to Zeus. Of course. Zahara might not have been totally wrong by saying that she didn't see a leader in me on that stage today. And while I might not be her idea of a leader, I'm sure as hell not a follower, either. I'm not Trevor. I wouldn't have handed my key over the second I crossed paths with Zeus, no matter what he promised me.

And neither would Alaric. Zeus has two keys because one

is Trevor's—his flunky. I release a shaky breath, embarrassed by how relieved I feel. I can't forget—it could be Alaric I'm facing down at the end of this thing. And while I can't imagine him fighting me, I also can't forget Zahara's words. She doesn't see me as a leader. Does Alaric?

"Ahhh, the little vamp," Zeus breathes. He is not looking well. Without his powers, Sora's attractiveness, and Rada's healing, his body is deteriorating fast. Sora would have been handsome even without his power but now I can see the imperfections that everyone has. His nose was a little crooked, his eyes a little close together, his skin sallow.

I guess the poor complexion could also be from the whole zombie thing. Speaking of which, my hair isn't the only thing the humidity is destroying. Zeus has several pieces of skin hanging off his body. He's missing a patch of flesh from his cheek and his jaw and teeth are visible.

"Well, you look like hot garbage," Sophia tells him.

Zeus laughs and maggots fall from the hole in his face. I try not to retch.

"As if you can talk. Oh, did the gods forget your sunscreen? Hmmm, maybe I do still have a few friends amongst the gods who made sure it got lost along the way…"

Zeus is cheating. I should have known. We're all stripped of our powers, and while I only had his strength for a short time, I already miss it. He's been alive since forever and always been all-powerful. Now he's just a former-god, and a half rotting one, at that. Technically, he's at the biggest disadvantage of all…but Hades and Hermes have spent their whole lives doing what Zeus says, and like Mama always said, the only thing harder to break than a hymen is a habit. If those guys found a way to give their old boss an edge, they'd take it.

And I can't just leave Sophia there to fight them herself. She might be a bitchy vampire, but she's *my* bitchy vampire.

I'm about to blow my cover when a hand grabs mine. I jump and turn to find my Mom. She wraps both arms tight around my arm and squeezes with all her weird zombie strength. It hurts.

"I'll rip this arm out before I let you sacrifice yourself for the competition."

There's an intense look in Mama's eyes. One I know too well. It's the "Mama don't bluff" look.

I gulp. Nod. And stay where I am.

"Hey, how did she get a knife?" Trevor is saying. He leans in to unstrap it from Sophia's leg when she bares her fangs, sinking them into his shoulder. He howls and falls over backwards.

"You bitch!" he shouts.

Sophia spits out a bit of flesh. "I must be dying," she tells him. "I was aiming for your neck."

"I'm bitten!" Trevor screams. "I'm going to turn into some crazy vamp fae hybrid. Can you imagine?!"

"Shut up, mortal," Zeus tells him. "It takes more than a bite to turn you into a vampire." Zeus pushes Trevor away and goes to Sophia, grabbing her by the neck and holding her up. "Give me your key or I will take it from your dead body."

She hisses at him and he drags her to the sunlight. "Give me your key," he repeats.

I want to go to her but what can I do? Without my super strength I'm just human. I can't save her. I can't save anyone.

Not Shauna, my post-apoc bestie who was taken by a creepy motorcycle gang.

Not Rada who Zeus killed right in front of me, while I just stared at him like a dummy.

And now I'm going to stand by and watch him kill Sophia too.

Maybe Zahara was right. I have no business being queen of the gods.

Zeus still has Sophia by the neck, but she's not going down without a fight. She brings her leg up high enough to unsheathe the blade and in one swoop she cuts off Zeus' hand, the weak zombie flesh giving way like butter.

Sophia laughs as she drops to the ground. She's directly in the sun now and her skin sizzles. She spits at Zeus as he pries the knife from her with his other hand and tosses it away.

"Help me," he commands Trevor.

Zeus is staring at the blackish-red blood pumping from the end of his stump, clearly shocked to be bleeding at all.

Trevor looks at Zeus, then at the fantastic amount of blood flowing out of him. Then Trevor leans against a tree with his arms crossed over his chest. "You seem to have it under control there, big guy. I don't want to get in your way."

Zeus glares at Trevor. "When I said earlier that I'd kill you if you got in my way, I didn't mean when I need help!"

Trevor smiles. "Just the same, I'd rather play it safe."

"That's ridiculous!" Zeus throws his hands up in the air, well, one hand and one stump, anyway. The other is still lying on the ground. But Trevor is unmoved. Did it just now occur to him that Zeus might not be the big swinging dick he used to be? Is Trevor hedging his bets?

"What good is it having a sidekick if they just stand around and watch?" Grumbling under his breath, Zeus moves Sophia by himself.

It would almost be funny, like some sort of weird buddy comedy. Except that they're both murderous and awful.

I'd almost forgotten Mama was beside me, until she whispers, "That boy is a strategist. He's working old Zeus."

I was thinking the same thing.

Confirming our suspicions, we both watch as Trevor darts forward to pocket Sophia's knife while Zeus drags Sophia into the sunlight.

Mama chuckles softly. "Oh yeah, someone's gonna end up

with that planted in their back."

Sophia hisses and fights Zeus even as the full force of the sun hits her body. She gets one more swipe in, raking her nails across his cheek, before suddenly disintegrating into ash with a soft poof.

"One down!" Zeus cheers, but it's clear he's hurting as he falls to his knees and starts to sift through Sophia's remains. "Her key isn't here!" he yells. He looks like he's about to pop a blood vessel.

"One of the others must have gotten to her first," Trevor says.

"Let's find them." Zeus slowly gets back to his feet. "This one was more trouble than she was worth." He kicks at the ash pile that was Sophia.

They move back into the trees and Zeus' voice once again fills the island. "LITTLE LION, LITTLE HARPY, LITTLE BEAUTY QUEEN..." His voice is menacing, but he's lost a lot of blood, and it doesn't carry the way it did before. It doesn't help that he stops and turns to Trevor.

"What rhymes with Queen?"

"Um...teen?" Trevor offers.

"No, that doesn't work!" Zeus scoffs. "I need something scary. Like earlier I said, *little fae, come out and play*. See?"

"Yeah," Trevor says. "But I can't come up with anything that rhymes with queen."

"What about lion?" Zeus asks.

"Um...that's even harder," Trevor says.

"No, wait," Zeus reaches out, his stumpy forearm brushing against Trevor's chest and leaving a smear of blackish zombie blood behind. "I've got it! LITTLE LION, I SET YOUR VAMPIRE FRIEND A-FRYING."

"See?" Zeus says, their voices fading as they make their way downstream. "You give up too easy, Trevor. Now do one for harpy."

6

———

"That one is all talk," Mama scoffs as Zeus' voice grows fainter.

"Mama!" I exclaim, turning to face her. "What are you doing here?"

"Brandee Jean, did you really think I would leave you out here alone?" She reaches up and adjusts my crown slightly, so it sits a little higher on my head. "Now you've done real good getting where you are now, but it's gonna take Mama's expertise to bring this one home." Grabbing my chin in her hand, Mama brings my face down to hers. "And no more helping the competition. You hear me?"

I pull away from her, my stomach churning.

Mama was always a little more cutthroat than me. Sure, I liked to win. But if another contestant ripped her nylons and I had a spare pair, I wouldn't hesitate to give them away. Mama said that type of thing was "shooting myself in the foot," not to mention costing us a pair of nylons. As I got older, I stopped doing those types of things...at least when Mama was watching.

Now though, with the reward so high and actual lives at

stake...I'm gonna have to finally decide if I want to do things my way or Mama's way.

Maybe Mama's way is the route to victory.

I keep trying to be everybody's friend and so far all it's gotten me is Zahara promising not to scar my face when she finally beats me.

"I hear you, Mama," I say at last. "I want to win this thing and...maybe it is time that I toughen up, instead of just acting tough."

Mama grins and the effect is scary; her teeth must not be sitting firm in her gums anymore 'cause they jut out at funny angles. "That's my girl."

Water laps at my feet again. I sigh and once again move toward higher land, with Mama following. "I still don't understand how you're here."

"Oh, Hades pointed me in the right direction," Mama says lightly.

I know my Mama and I know when she says a man's name in the tone she just said "Hades" that I'm gonna have to crank my white noise machine at night during future "sleepovers."

"You're hooking up with Hades!?"

"Mind your mouth, Brandee Jean!" Mama snaps. "Hades and I...we have an understanding." She giggles softly, almost to herself. "He's an amazing man. Strong. Powerful." She frowns. "Of course, he still wants his big brother to win this thing. But I'm helping him see that Zee doesn't consider him an equal. Hades will always be an underling if Zeus is in charge again. But you, BJ, would do things differently. Especially if Hades was your new daddy."

"Oh gods," I say.

"I know, baby. It's the happy ending I always dreamed of for us."

"Really?"

Mama doesn't know how not on board I am with this whole plan. Or maybe, just like with Hades, she figures that I'll be brought around to her point of view eventually. She always said she'd do anything for her little girl, and I knew she meant it when she banged the whole panel of judges for the Miss Mountaineer contest. Even the lady judges.

"Now, look," Mama says fishing around in the pocket of her skin-tight jeans. "I heard that most of this island was going to basically be underwater for large chunks of time and knew I needed to get you some help. I really should have gotten you those swim lessons, but it was that or paying for flippers when your baby teeth were coming out, and well that was an easy choice. I couldn't let my girl have holes in her smile."

She grins at me, once again showing off the horrific gaping holes in her own mouth.

"It's okay, Mama. You did what you had to at the time—"

I stop abruptly as Mama pulls my secret weapon from her pocket. I was hoping for some arm floaties. Or maybe a snorkel. Instead, she hands me a tube of Xtra Tough Waterproof Mascara.

"Here we go," she says removing the cap. "You can't compete with raccoon eyes."

She gestures for me to lean forward and too weary to argue, I do it. Tilting my head this way and that, she layers the mascara on until I can feel the weight of it on my eyelids.

Finally satisfied, she steps back. "Okay, I gotta get back. Hades didn't want me to be discovered and have all the other gods up his ass for breaking the rules again." Mama rolls her eyes like expecting him to follow the rules is unreasonable.

"Wait," I say, as she hands me the tube of mascara. "How are you getting back?"

"There's a portal hidden on the ocean floor not far off the

island. The saltwater isn't great for my skin, so I can't be popping back and forth."

She turns and walks toward the shore. The water is so high, she has to wade through it. Before disappearing beneath the tide, she looks back, "Knock 'em dead, baby girl. And I do mean that literally."

"Bye, Mama!" I stand at the edge of the water and wave until she dives under, a decent chunk of her scalp coming up to the surface after she's gone. I don't know how rough Hades likes his women, but Mama might not be warming his bed for much longer. I guess I need to take advantage of every weapon I've got in my corner. And if that's waterproof mascara and Mama romancing Hades, well… I straighten my crown.

So far, I'm the only person on this island who has shown any reluctance to hurt people. I know Zahara offered to not maim me for life, but that was about as far as she was willing to go. I have no doubt Sophia would gladly have killed me if she wasn't already looking like a bucket of extra crispy fried chicken when we met up. Trevor and Zeus are so excited to kill me that they're busting rhymes about it. Malik has always had a glint in his eye, even when he wasn't shifted into a lion. I have no doubt he'd kill to get these keys off me.

And Alaric…

I shake my head, the crown holding firmly in place, along with the key, in my teased locks. I can't say what Alaric would do.

Probably the noble thing. Probably the right thing.

But is having a weak Midwestern beauty pageant teenager in charge of the world the right thing?

From across the island I hear a voice, carried on the wind. "COME OUT LITTLE HARPY, SO I CAN FEED YOU TO THE CARP-Y."

Well…the world might not thank me for it, but I'm still going to take a shot at running it.

I slip Sophia's key into my mile-high hair, where the jade clinks against the silver of my own key. Funny, I don't remember seeing Zahara's key. The get-up that they put us in for this island adventure doesn't leave a lot of room for hiding places. Where did that tricky little bird put hers? And was she purposely keeping me too distracted not to ask?

A shadow passes over me, and I look up to find Zahara gliding above, scanning the island. She veers suddenly as if she's spotted something, and I make a note of her direction. I might not have wings, but that doesn't mean I don't have a bird's eye view.

"I'm following your ass!" I scream at the sky, and she changes direction again, spinning back toward me. I'm not assuming she's going to give me a friendly warning again; I duck for cover, just in time. A big, wet turd splats onto the sand right where I'd been standing. Her laughter rings in the air for a long time after her shadow is gone.

I only come out once I know it's safe. Zahara might have some natural advantages, but so do I. These legs didn't win the No-Shave November contest for nothing. There's muscle underneath all this spray tan, and I could walk across this island five times without needing a rest. But the tide lapping at my heels as I start out at a jog reminds me…I still can't swim.

I stick to the stream, although I keep my nose pointed in the direction I saw Zahara go. The gods might have remembered to give me a canteen, but that doesn't mean water will always be easy to find. After seeing Sophia go up in a poof of ash, I'm not in a hurry to get dehydrated. Plus, whenever I miss out on my eight glasses of water a day, my skin loses its winning glow.

Funny thing, though, this stream is broken. I didn't think about it the first time I filled my canteen; Zahara landing on me from above had my attention. But the second time I refill, I notice something is off. The current is going the wrong way. Mama didn't always get every saying right, but she did have one that she usually remembered—all rivers lead to the sea. What she meant by that is that even dingy little competitions like Miss Upper Peninsula Upholstery Queen (we all had to make our dresses out of curtains) would eventually pave the route to Miss American Miss.

But this river isn't leading to the sea; it's going the opposite direction. I screw the lid back onto my canteen and retrace my steps to double check. Yep, the tide is still coming in—and from what Mama said it sounds like it's not going to stop. But this river is going inward, just like me. I splash along beside it for a bit, keeping my eyes open for a weapon. Sophia had said I might find one, the way she did her knife, but I haven't seen anything yet.

The only accessory I've got is this crown, and while I appreciate it as a thing of beauty, I might need something pointier soon. I'm considering how bad things gotta get for me to consider breaking a filigree from my crown and sharpening it against a rock.

The idea of it makes me want to cry, but desperate times call for desperate measures. That's what Mama said the time we were behind on our rent payment and the only contest with a cash prize was for Miss Good Grease. It was a cooking oil company sponsoring it, so Mama coated me up from my hair roots to the tips of my painted toes. If we'd got into a car crash on the way there I woulda slipped right through the seat belt.

Suddenly I become aware of a faint roaring sound. Like a

lion letting everyone know he's ready to play. Immediately I duck down behind a rock, my hand going to my crown, protectively. Once, I was in a Miss Hide and Sneak Laser Tag pageant, where one girl started with the crown, and the others hunted her down. You were supposed to give up the head gear if you got zapped, but nobody was real keen on that rule. We quickly ditched the laser guns and used the weapons the good lord had given us—our fingernails. They had to cut the live feed from that particular broadcast due to the gruesome nature of the scalp injuries.

It's like that now. My pulse is racing. My muscles clenched. My fingers curled around my crown.

"Screw you, Zahara," I say, under my breath. I might not be a leader, but this is my crown. And if I'm right and that roaring sound is Malik, I'm about to find out what I'm willing to do to keep it.

7

─────

I'm crouched, ready to fight a lion, when I realize that the roaring sound isn't getting any closer. Or getting louder. It's staying exactly the same. I suddenly realize that what I hear isn't Malik after all. It's a waterfall.

I get to my feet and follow the stream again, noticing that the current has picked up. There's stuff floating in it now, getting caught up in a rapidly increasing flow. I spot Zeus' hand that Sophia lopped off for him, branches from a tree, and a length of rope.

Ha! Rope might be just what Brandee Jean ordered. If I want to get out of this without killing anyone, I'm either going to have to convince everyone that I'm the rightful Amazon Queen of the Gods…or, I can just convince one or two of them and then tie the rest up and take their keys.

I'm so excited about not having to kill anybody that I wade right into the current, forgetting the whole "fast water is dangerous" thing. My feet can touch, that's all I know. Or at least, they can touch until they're knocked right out from under me.

Brandee Jean never was much of an outdoorsy girl.

I lose sight of the rope and am dragged under. I come back up, gulping for air, one hand snatching at brush on the sides of the river, the other madly jammed onto the wet mop that is my hair—and a crown, plus two keys to win the world.

Deciding the keys are more important than dragging myself out of the water, I give up trying to hold onto anything other than what's on my head. Wherever this river is going, I am too. I just have to not drown before I get there.

My feet are kicking and I manage to hit bottom, push up, gulp air, then get rolled back under the surface once more. I kick again, searching for footing. I push for the surface once more and as my head breaks water, see the absolute worst thing ever: the end of the road.

"Oh shiiiiiiiiiiiiiit!" I yell, just as the river breaks over the edge of a canyon.

I go over with it and I'm riding the wave of a waterfall. Mama may not have paid for swimming lessons, but she said a graceful girl should always know how to swan dive. So she put a ladder next to an inflatable yard pool and told me not to break my neck one summer during the Olympics. All we watched was diving, and I got pretty good at diving without knowing how to swim, or cracking my skull open in five feet of water.

My training kicks in and I'm spiraling through space, my stomach in my throat, my heart in my feet, and my hands in my hair.

I'm way higher than that yard pool. Way. But luckily the lagoon beneath me is a lot deeper than five feet.

I'm surrounded by endless blue, and I have no idea which way is up. Is this what flying is like? If I could only push off the bottom...or float to the top? Shouldn't my boobs work as flotation devices in case of an emergency? I mean, so far in life they've served as decoration only. Isn't it time they contributed?

I'm still sinking, scrambling wildly as my limbs mimic what I think might be swimming movements. But really I'm just clawing at the lagoon water, the pressure of the falls pushing me back down. I've got to get out from under this waterfall...but I can't. I don't know how. My lungs are screaming, wanting to open, begging me to take a breath, even though the only thing I'll be pulling in is water.

All the blue in my vision is going black and in one last panicked attempt to not drown I release my breath. A bubble floats past my lips, and I watch it rise to the surface, doing exactly what I need to do, but don't know how. This is it. I'm done. Drowned at the bottom of a lagoon on a magical island. At least I have my crown, and I'll make a nice-looking corpse. Oh gods, unless Hades brings me back as a zombie. Him and Mama and me could be a whole little underworld family.

It's my last thought.

And then someone is sitting on my chest. No, not sitting, pushing. I feel lips on mine. Gentle. Strong. Breathing? This is the weirdest kiss ever. Oh shit, did Hades already find my bloated body? Is this the afterlife? If some wanna-be Prince Charming thinks this is the way to wake a girl, I'm gonna rip his lips off.

I'm suddenly completely awake and puking up water. It's warm as it slips past my lips, which means it's been in my lungs awhile. I've been dead for...well, long enough to warm up lagoon water with my body heat. Gulping in a breath full of wonderful air, I cough and try to get up, but I'm super light-headed.

"Calm down," a familiar voice tells me. "You came bloody close to drowning and then spewed up half the lagoon."

I turn to find myself staring into the eyes of Alaric.

"Actually, I think I did drown. Or at least, mostly drowned. You saved me?" I ask.

He shrugs. "It appears that I did." He abruptly stands so that he's towering over me. I blink and scrub water out of my eyes. But no, my first glance was correct. He's glaring at me. Alaric is pissed. "I saw your swan dive. Quite impressive form. But then when you didn't come up...I dove under three different times searching for you." He drags a hand through his own soaked hair. "Finally, on the last time." A shuddering breath escapes Alaric and it occurs to me that maybe he isn't simply pissed. Maybe he was scared.

"I don't know how to swim," I tell him, a little sheepishly.

His eyes nearly bug out of his head. "You what?!? Have you completely lost the plot, Brandee Jean? Why were you diving into the lagoon if you can't swim?"

"I didn't mean to, I was swept along and then there I was falling and well, I decided to do it with style."

Speaking of style...I'm suddenly glad my mama brought me waterproof mascara, although I probably look like a drenched poodle anyway. My hands go immediately to my head, but the keys are still there, hopelessly entangled in my hair.

Alaric watches me, some of the starchiness draining out of him. A small smile plays across his mouth as he asks, "Worried about your hair, in this situation?"

I stand, try to look offended, but that's hard when someone just saved your life. Especially when it would have benefited them to let you die. And also, when that person is super cute in a stuffy English lord kind of way, and has an awesome accent, it's just really hard to do anything other than feel a little weak in the knees. Or maybe that's because I was dead for a little bit there.

"Why?" I ask. "Why did you save me?"

He frowns again. "You think I'd just stand here and let

you drown? Toodle pip, Brandee Jean, it was nice knowing you."

"No, I guess not. It's just...Zeus killed Sophia. Trevor watched. Zahara told me that if it comes down to the two of us, I'm hamburger. And Malik..." I pause. "I haven't even spotted him yet. For all I know Zeus already got to him."

"I'm right here," a voice tells me. I spin to find Malik...in a loincloth. It's not a bad sight, but my heart goes up into my throat anyway.

"Malik and I have formed a temporary alliance," Alaric explains. "We're going to try and bring down the others..."

"I'm an other," I whisper.

"Don't worry," Malik grins. "It was part of our truce that if we found you, you'd be given the option to join. Fae boy here was very adamant. He said without me agreeing to include you, he wouldn't align with me."

I look at Alaric. "Really?" I ask.

"Yeah, that boy has it bad for you," Malik tells me. "I mean, if he was the one in a loincloth we'd probably have an embarrassing moment on our hands right now."

Alaric blushes, but then helps me to my feet. I don't need Malik to inform me about a potential loincloth situation; I was stuck in a time out box with Alaric not that long ago. Quarters were close, and from that brief encounter I'm pretty sure Alaric would need an XL loincloth.

"It just makes sense for us to unite," Alaric explains. "Trevor and Zeus are together. Zahara can fly. Creating a strong alliance will help us get on top."

"Bro, you were totally on top of her," Malik tells him. "If I win this, first thing I'm doing is signing up for CPR classes. That was hot."

I'm shaky on my feet but I'm glad I'm with people I can trust—for the moment at least. "And when it's just the three of us?" I ask.

"Rock, scissors, paper," Malik tells me.

"I never agreed to that rubbish idea," Alaric says with a grimace.

"Would you rather fight it out to the death?" Malik asks. "Cause I'm pretty sure lion beats faerie. And I've never even seen you do anything fae-ish. Your supernatural blood must be pretty thin."

"Let's focus on survival right now and making sure we're the last three standing. Once we get there, we'll discuss next steps." Alaric neatly sidesteps the question about the amount of fae blood he has in him.

"Are you in?" Malik asks and after a final moment of hesitation I nod.

"But can I ask...what is going on with the loincloth?"

Malik looks down. "Oh, this? Well they didn't give us magically shifting clothes, so when I turned into my lion form I busted out of the Indiana Jones get up. I think I look good like this, though." He flexes. "Sexy, right?"

I smile. "You do have the legs for it."

"Come on, we have to show you something." He bounds off and I follow, Alaric putting an arm around me to help hold me upright. I lean into him and let him carry some of my weight.

It feels beyond nice.

8

"**Z**eus killed Sophia?" Alaric asks, breaking the silence and my warm and fuzzy moment.

"Yeah, it was terrible," I tell him. "She fought hard till the end, though."

"That means Zeus has at least three keys now."

I shake my head. "No, last I saw he only had his and Trevor's, and it looks like Trevor is getting more and more fed up with being Zeus' lackey."

"So who has Sophia's key?"

I wink at him. "Me."

"You have it?" he asks, scanning my body. I feel like he's not checking out the goods. This is purely business, and I'm a little hurt.

"It's safe," I assure him. "Are you really going to play a game to determine who wins at the end if it's just us left?" I ask.

"This whole competition has been a game." He's not wrong. "Although rock paper scissors may be anticlimactic, and lacking in dignity, I have to admit that I can't think of any better way to stick it in the gods' faces than to make their ultimate prize into a joke."

I think about it for a second, remembering the glare in Sophia's eyes when she held up her key, wanting me and Zahara to fight for it. We had both laughed, and even through all her pain, I could see her confusion. The gods know power, and they treasure it. So did Sophia, with her royal vampire blood.

Alaric's right. We have been playing the gods' game all along, fighting for a prize they think is worthwhile.

But what do I treasure? What about Malik? Or Alaric? Sure, it's easy enough to say we're all friends now, but once it's down to the nitty-gritty, will they both hold to that?

Mama always says there's more than one way to skin someone on the catwalk. I guess I gotta figure out what that might be when and if it gets down to just us three.

"We're here!" Malik calls back to us. "I shifted as soon as I got here, crisscrossed the island to get a feel for the terrain."

"I'm pretty sure this is the puzzle we're all supposed to be working towards solving," Alaric adds. "Plus, it's at the geographical center of the island, and the tide is pushing us all inward. They want us to find this."

It'd be pretty hard to miss, honestly. Before us looms a statue on a stone base taller than I am. It's at least fifty feet tall, sexless and faceless. There is a crown that looks a lot like the one I'm wearing and a massive sword sheathed at its side.

"Who is it?" I ask.

"We've been discussing that," Alaric tells me.

"We think it's like, us," Malik says. "Whoever is gonna win. Insert your face here."

"There's an inscription." Alaric points to it.

"What does it say?"

"My ancient Greek is a little rusty..." Alaric looks sheepish.

"He means non-existent," Malik clarifies.

"I studied Latin," Alaric huffs. "I can't learn every dead language…"

"What's this?" I ask studying the base. There's foliage covering most of it but I scrape it away. "It looks like a keyhole."

Malik and Alaric both help me remove the plants around the stone base and we find more keyholes. "This one is Jade," Malik calls.

"And this one diamond," I say.

"My key is diamond!" Malik says.

Damn…why couldn't I get a diamond key? That would be rocking in my updo.

"Okay, we have different keys that match these keyholes." Can it be that easy? Play a matching game and win the world?

"That's not much of a puzzle," Alaric confirms.

"Maybe the gods are super over this competition," I say. "Maybe they're just phoning it in."

"Or maybe it's a trick," Alaric whispers so only I can hear. "They wouldn't mess around with the next ruler of the gods."

"I heard Zeus say that quite a few were still on his side. That winged feet guy…"

"Hermes," Alaric interrupts.

"Right, Hermes, is on his side, but I think Hades is running more lukewarm these days."

"What makes you think that?" Alaric asks.

"Hey, what are you two plotting?" Malik asks. "I see how it is, Miss big boobs comes along and now I'm out? What happened to bros before hos?"

"No one is out," Alaric tells him. "Our truce holds."

"Yeah, we're just a threesome now," I say. "Ménage à trois. See, you're not the only one with some foreign language."

"I can totally get behind that...except I always pictured two girls, not..."

"Hey, I'm in! Second girl accounted for!" a figure from the top of the statue calls down to us. Zahara.

"What do you want, harpy?" Alaric asks.

"Well, if you're not serious about the group sex, just to rest for a moment," she tells us. "And scope out the competition."

"You can rest anywhere," Malik tells her. "Get lost or I'm going to shift, climb up there, and have a nice harpy dinner."

"Charming," Zahara stretches her wings. "I actually *can't* rest anywhere else. The tide came in and this is the highest spot around."

"The gods planned this to push us all together," Alaric says. "Make us fight."

"Wait, then that means..." I twirl around, scanning the different streams and inlets that filter into the canyon. Sure enough, I spot some splashing, and Trevor climbs onto the bank a hundred yards away, dropping into a crouch when he sees us.

"Where's Zeus?" Malik yells.

"Oh, he's there," Zahara calls, pointing past Trevor, where a mer-tail flicks up. "He's in Sora's body, remember?"

"And Sora's a damn merman," Alaric says under his breath.

"No fair!" I yell up at Zahara. "You've got wings to fly to safety and Zeus can breathe underwater!"

"Hey, I didn't make the rules, or the playing field," Zahara shrugs. "Hand over your keys and I'll bring you up here with me."

"Don't do it!" Malik says, and I nod in agreement, but not before my hands go protectively to my hair. His dark eyes follow the movement, calculating. I take a step closer to Alaric, tucking my arm under his elbow.

Suddenly, a loud rumble fills the air, and water begins to fill the canyon from all sides, running over the lip and crashing to the canyon floor. The tide is here, and it's going to drown us all.

9

———

"Run!" Malik screams, but there's nowhere to flee. We can't climb the sides of the rocky walls of the valley, not with the water pouring down. There are some trees still above the tide, but who knows how long they will remain above water. The statue is by far the tallest thing down around—and there's a harpy in fight mode perched on top of it.

Malik glances at Alaric and me. "Best of luck," he says, then shifts into a lion and leaps onto the statue. But his claws can't find much purchase on the smooth stone, and he slips backwards a few feet for every one that he gains.

"Go!" Alaric says, the roar of the water now filling our ears, the spray in my face. The ocean is filling the canyon, and he might have saved me from the lagoon just to see me drown in saltwater. I run for a tree, splashing through the shallows, well aware that no matter how high I can climb, the water will rise higher.

Alaric is right behind me, giving my rear a helpful push when I slip. "Don't look down!" He calls, but I do anyway, to see that Trevor is happily backstroking around the base of the tree, smiling.

"He was an alternate for the Olympic swim team," Alaric informs me, sweat dripping from his brow. "This place was practically made for him."

"Well, that's some bullshit," I say through my teeth, grabbing for the next branch just as Zeus' merman tail flicks again, splashing Trevor playfully.

I get as high as I can before the branches won't hold me anymore, and Alaric joins me. We watch as the water rises, and Malik scrambles up the statue. Zahara leans over the edge, eyeing him. She takes to wing, giving him a fly by. Her voice carries.

"Give it up, lion man," she calls. "You can't hold on much longer."

It's true. Malik's lion muscles are quivering with exertion, the diamond key dangling from his loincloth catching the light as it swings. He snarls at her, but it's a mistake, and a waste of energy. He slides another few feet, leaving claw marks behind.

Zeus surfaces, glaring. "Hey! Don't mark up my statue! That's going to be my pretty face up there, kid!"

But Malik doesn't have the chance to answer. He's holding on for dear life. Zahara swoops past again, her tone no longer teasing.

"Malik!" she yells. "Don't be stupid! Toss me your key and I'll take you to the top. If you concede, you don't have to die!"

"No," Zeus yells. "You don't! But I'll gladly kill you!" He dives again, and circles the statue, his tail flicking up and down in delight. Trevor laughs, rolls over onto his back to float while humming the theme from *Jaws*. "Duh duh. Duh duh. Duh duh duh duh duh duh."

We're in the highest branch that will hold us, but the

water is licking at my ankles now. I cling to Alaric, who eyes the water below.

"This won't stop rising. We'll have to tread water."

I hug him more tightly. "I don't know how to do that! What part of 'I can't swim' did you not understand earlier?"

"Not at all?" he asks.

"I literally drowned ten minutes ago," I say. "That's how much I *can't* swim."

There's a scream from the statue, and I look over in time to see Malik lose his grip, his lion body twisting and turning as he falls, looking for purchase in midair. Zahara dives, tries to catch him, but misses. Zeus surfaces, and Trevor points.

"There! He fell there!" he yells, and Zeus goes under again, madly swimming to where Malik hit the water. It's churning, roiling from the constant influx from the water pouring over the canyon rim from both sides. Malik rises above the water just once, his whiskers dripping. His eyes meet mine and I yell, reaching for him even though he's impossibly far away.

"Zahara!" I scream, pointing a finger his way, knowing she won't let him die.

But she's not any closer than me. She swoops toward him, close to the rising water.

She's nearly to Malik when he goes under once more.

Her claws dip into the water, but come up empty.

Malik is gone.

10

"Malik!" I yell, but I know it's too late. Even if cats were great swimmers, merman-Zeus is patrolling the waters, and I have no doubt he'll drown Malik without regret. Zahara returns to her perch on top of the statue, watching as Zeus and Trevor scout the water for Malik's body.

"BJ," Alaric says, his eyes bright and intense. "I'm going to teach you how to swim."

"Right now?" I ask, which gets a thin smile out of him.

"Can you think of a better time?"

I laugh. I can't help it. We're about to die, and this guy can still make me laugh. Mama always says a boy that can make you laugh is a keeper. Of course she also said that if he has a dick over eight inches, you can overlook a lot of personality flaws.

"Brandee, can you ride a bike?" Alaric asks.

"Yeah, but those don't float," I tell him. "And I don't have one on me."

"Sure, but you know how, right?"

"Um, do you think these quads made themselves?" I

ask him.

"I'll take that as a yes," Alaric says, letting go of the branch to slip down into the water. It's calmer now, the tide no longer rushing in from the lips of the canyon. Poor Malik, if he'd only been able to climb a few more feet…

But calmer water or not, it can still drown me if I can't swim. Alaric bobs in front of me, holding his hands out. "Brandee, all you have to do is pump those legs like you're in the Tour de France."

"Is that a sports thing?" I ask.

"Bike race," he says. "Just act like you're on a bike, trying to win a race. It's called treading water." We lock eyes, and I slide into the water, kicking madly.

"Oh my gods!" I say, as I stay afloat. "I'm swimming."

Alaric grimaces. "Well, kind of."

"Hey, I'm not drowning!" I argue, just as Malik's lion corpse surfaces next to me. I scream, lose my rhythm, and immediately begin to sink. I grab onto the first thing I can find—a dead lion—but it's immediately tugged from under my grasp. Underwater, Zeus grins toothily, and swims away, towing Malik's corpse behind.

I ride my invisible water bike like crazy, and my head breaks the surface.

"Zeus grabbed Malik," I tell Alaric. And suddenly, Trevor bobs between us.

"Hey losers," he says. "Which one of you should I drown first? Maybe the one with two keys?" He eyes me, and I ride that bike like Lance Armstrong. If Trevor gets anywhere near me, he'll catch a few shots to the groin before I go out.

"Or should I go for brother dear?" Trevor asks, turning to Alaric.

Zahara swoops down, and I think she's coming in to pluck me from the water, but instead her talons rake my hair as she does a pass.

"Hey!" I scream up at her. "Watch it!"

"I am," she yells, circling past. "Those keys in your hair catch the sun nicely. Toss them to me, and I'll take you to safety."

I tread water, considering. That's the same deal she offered Malik, and now he's dead.

"Don't do it, BJ," Alaric says to me, but his eyes are still on his half-brother, ready for a lunge. "You can tread water for a while, and the water isn't rising anymore."

He's right. The tide isn't coming over the lip of the canyon any longer, which means it must act like a normal tide in at least one sense: it recedes. Good to know. Suddenly, there's a popping sound, like suction being broken, and I feel a tug at my legs.

"What's happening now?" I ask, just as the pull becomes stronger. Alaric lunges for me, grabbing me around the waist and holding onto a tree branch just as Zahara flies back to her perch, eyeing the water around us as the level starts to drop rapidly. Trevor is swept past us, his brow furrowed as he swims madly against the pull. Zeus surfaces near the canyon wall, yelling in frustration at Trevor.

"Do you see the body? I lost my grip on it!"

"What?!" Trevor yells back. "You had one job!"

"And I only have one hand!" Zeus yells back, then dives underwater again, presumably looking for Malik's corpse, and the diamond key still dangling from the loincloth.

"What's going on?" I ask Alaric, as he pulls me up alongside him. I wrap both arms around the branch, holding on like Miss Alabama did to her crown the one time she didn't let the judges finish pronouncing "Alaska" before she jumped for the goods.

"The canyon is draining," Alaric says. "The gods must have designed it that way. There are probably caves leading out to sea that they magically block until they want the water out of the canyon."

Even as Alaric talks, the water goes out so fast we're suddenly clinging to the weak branches at the tippy top of the tree that's now only halfway underwater. We both shimmy down the tree until we're just above the waterline.

I sit with the trunk at my back, my legs dangling down so the water laps my toes. "You know, this reminds me of the Miss Winter Wonderland contest a few years back," I tell Alaric as he sits down facing me. "The director had a nervous breakdown and decided to hose down one of the outdoor paths we were using for the swimsuit catwalk. As if it wasn't bad enough being out in ten-degree weather in a bikini, we all went slipping and sliding all over the place in our high heels. One girl even broke her leg. The director swore she was just trying to make it more winter-like, but it was pretty clear when she was laughing so hard she pissed herself. She was messing with us."

"It might be the stress, but that story does seem appropriate to this situation," Alaric says.

I nod, glad to know Alaric is seeing the value in my beauty pageant wisdom. "You think the gods are having a nervous breakdown?"

"I don't know, Brandee," Alaric says with a shrug. "I stopped trying to figure out what the gods want a long time ago."

"Oh yeah?" I ask. "Then what are you trying to figure out?"

He looks at me, his mouth suddenly a very serious, very British straight line. "What *I* want," he says.

Then he pulls me closer, and kisses me.

It's not often a girl gets kissed so good she forgets that she's stuck in a tree to keep from drowning and that the boy swapping spit with her also has good reason to kill her.

But all of it goes right outta my head.

The contest. The prize. The cost of losing.

I don't even think about my appearance, which pretty much never happens. Even when Alaric's hands are in my hair, all I'm thinking is how good it feels to have his fingertips massaging my scalp where that damn crown had been digging into—

I jerk back with a screech and nearly fall right out of the tree. All that's left of the water is puddles, which means I mighta broken my neck. Of course, that might've been preferable to being stuck with this snake.

"How could you?" I demand of Alaric, who now holds both of my keys in his big hand.

"Do you seriously take me for the dodgy type of bloke who would nick your keys?"

"What does that mean? Are you talking in Latin or something?" Frustrated, I take a swing at him, but he easily leans away. "Just give me my keys back!"

"No. Securing them in your hair was complete tosh. Look how easily I got them away from you. I'm trying to prove a point."

"If tosh means brilliant, then yes it was. And besides, it's not like I'm going to let Trevor or Zeus kiss me—" Ew. I throw up a little bit in my mouth, cutting off my own words.

"Everyone has seen them, Brandee Jean! And they don't have to kiss you to get them. Do you want to be scalped by Zahara?"

This gives me pause. To lose the keys would be terrible. But to also be stripped of my hair…

I'm not sure I could survive that.

"Fine," I mutter. "But you could've just told me. You didn't have to just take them. Especially when we were kissing. Didn't that mean nothing to you?"

Alaric's eyes go dark. "Didn't mean nothing?" He sighs and shakes his head. "Yes, that's precisely what it meant."

My heart sinks at that. Alaric never struck me as a player. Or the sorta guy who would just casually kiss a girl to pass the time while stuck up in a tree. But maybe I was wrong about him.

Mama always said the only man you can trust is a woman. And even then, watch out, 'cause there are some nasty bitches.

To be totally honest, a lot of the time it seemed like Mama didn't really like anyone much except me. And her flavor of the month boyfriend. That's my mama; her love blazes bright and short. I hope her fling with Hades doesn't get her burned. If nothing else, it brought her back to me.

And I'm going to do my mama proud.

I snatch my keys back from Alaric and hide them down my shirt, tucked securely under my best assets. Alaric actually looks away as I fiddle. I do not understand this boy. One minute we're playing tonsil hockey and the next he's acting like a blushing virgin. I'm over it.

The tide has washed out of the valley, along with Zeus, Trevor, and Malik's body.

I shimmy down the tree.

"Brandee, where are you going?" Alaric calls down.

"I'm going to play this stupid game and maybe I'll decide that you'd make a better king, but I'm not gonna let someone else make that decision for me!" I yell up at him.

The ground squishes beneath my feet as I stomp through the mud left behind after all the water receded. Though I'm exhausted from treading water, I know I can't keep running away. I've gotta run toward something.

"I'm going to find that dirtbag Zeus," I say. "And I'm gonna punch him in Sora's pretty face."

11

———

I turn toward the caves, only a little surprised when Alaric follows, although a lot irritated with myself for being happy about it.

Do I want this stuck-up know-it-all boy on my heels—even if he is a good kisser? Yes.

Do I want him burying his fingers in my hair?

Yes, but not if he's only digging for what's mine. Yes, mine.

Crap, I'm thinking in terms of winning again, and that might not work out so well now that Malik—one third of our alliance—is dead. If it comes down to me and Alaric playing rock paper scissors for the crown, will I be able to accept it if I lose?

And more importantly, will he?

I can't think that far ahead right now. It's dumb to wonder how I'll react to winning *or* losing when I only have two keys, and those were taken so easily from me...even if I do have them back now.

"Brandee, wait," Alaric catches up to me, his hand on my

arm. I slide out from under his grasp, alarmed at how much I like his touch. "We're still a team," he says.

"Are we?" I ask, hands on my hips.

Alaric lifts up his shirt. For a moment all I can see is his broad chest and the muscles that make up his belly and the trail of dark hair that disappears down into his shorts…

With effort I pull my mind out of the gutter and instead focus on what he's trying to show me. Of course, Alaric isn't the type to show off his hot bod, which is a damn shame because he could really rock a muscle shirt if he wanted to. I suppose that's one of the many things he tends to think of as crass and improper.

Which means that flashing his pecs at me is his way of apologizing. Actually, showing me what's wrapped around those pecs is his way of apologizing. Rope, similar to the one I nearly drowned trying to reach, wraps around his middle, crisscrossed, and then loops over his shoulders.

I twirl a finger up in the air, indicating that Alaric should spin. Amazingly, despite looking embarrassed, he does I asks, slowly turning. The rope x's over his back, digging into the space beneath his shoulder blades. I can't resist taking a step forward to touch the reddened, rope-burned skin. He shudders as my fingers make contact.

"Brandee Jean," he says, spinning to face me once more. His voice is rough.

I trail my fingers across the rope where it finally ends in a complicated knot at the base of his rib cage. There, twisted into the knot, is his key.

"You got the ruby key," I say, unable to resist touching it. Or Alaric's warm skin. I press my hand against his heart, enjoying how frantically it beats against my palm.

Abruptly he steps back, jerking his shirt back down. "We haven't time for hanky panky. We're in danger and—" Alaric exhales roughly, then rakes his hands through his hair. "Look, are we square again?"

"Were you a Boy Scout?" I ask. "With the knots and stuff?"

"Er, no." He tugs at his collar. "Yachting club."

I roll my eyes. "I should've known."

"Right. That's done. What's our next step?"

"We've got to find Malik's body," I tell him. "Zeus couldn't hold onto it against the suction, which means that it got pulled into one of these caves when the canyon drained." I glance around the canyon floor, overwhelmed by the amount of black, yawning cave mouths I see all around us.

"You're probably right," Alaric says. "But I don't see Zeus or Trevor anywhere, and they didn't climb out. They're on the same track, and have a better idea of which cave mouth the body was closest to when Zeus lost it."

"So, they're ahead of us," I finish for him. Above, Zahara wheels in the sky, watching us intently. I shield my eyes against the sun. "Do you think she saw where they went?"

"Maybe," Alaric shrugs. "But do we trust her to tell us the truth if we ask?"

Even three hours ago, I might have said yes. But now…I don't know. "She's waiting to see what we do," I tell Alaric. "And she might have some natural advantages over us. Do harpies have any bat skills? Can she see in the dark?"

"I don't think that's true, Brandee Jean," Alaric says. "And I don't know if she can see in the dark, but she probably does have abilities that will be useful to her that we simply don't."

"Great, so the two clueless humans are teamed up against a god and a harpy."

"A former god," Alaric corrects. "And while being human might seem commonplace, I do have some useful skills."

He's a damn good kisser, for one thing, but I don't think that's what he's talking about. Then there's his knotting skills, which are tight. Plus if we come across a hidden yacht, he'll be all over that too. But I don't think that's what he's talking about.

I cross my arms. "Like what?"

"Common sense," he says, turning toward the canyon wall and the various cave openings.

"Think about it. Malik's body is gone, which means it was pulled into a cave. We can eliminate any openings he couldn't fit through right away."

"Duh," I say. "Also, we couldn't fit through them either so it's not like we were going to search them."

"I'm thinking aloud," Alaric says. "Please allow me that without interrupting."

Every time I warm up to him and think I'm about to fall for Alaric, he turns a cold British shoulder on me. Still, he's cute when he's thinking.

"Smaller holes would have more suction, though," Alaric says, walking towards the canyon wall, stones rolling out from under his boots. I follow, aware that Zahara is shadowing us from above.

"If we look in the area where we last saw Zeus, then find a cave entrance that's big enough to allow the body to pass through, but small enough to have more suction than a larger one nearby, we'll be on the right track."

Alaric stops at a cluster of cave mouths, rubbing his chin while he thinks. "Unfortunately, we have no way to truly measure the cave mouths, so we'll have to eyeball it. Which could be tricky."

"Or," I say, marching up to an entrance. "We can use our eyeballs in a different way that doesn't use math at all, and say—wow, look! Here's a big tuft of lion hair. Wonder where that came from?"

I pick up the clump of hair. It's wet and matted, and my joking tone drops entirely as I roll it in my fingers. This came off Malik's dead body. We can't forget that what we're doing is dangerous, and that while nobody necessarily has to die, so far the two people that were eliminated have taken that route. Alaric and I might be planning on sticking it to the gods by deciding who wins the big prize with a child's game, but everyone else here cares enough to die—and to kill —for it."

Alaric moves closer, sensing my mood. "Good find, Brandee," he says.

I let go of Malik's fur and it is picked up by the wind, tumbling away in the breeze. "How do we know that Zeus and Trevor aren't in there already? How do we know that we're not about to wander into a dark place where they can ambush us?"

Alaric peers into the cave, his mouth downturned. "We don't."

———

These caves suck.

And no, I don't just mean like they have suction for draining water from a canyon. They suck in the sense that everything is wet, dark, cold, and also, creepy as shit.

It doesn't help that we're on the search for a corpse and might possibly walk right into the arms of a former god in a rotting body, not to mention Alaric's murderous bastard brother.

"Any ideas on how to make light?" I ask Alaric, when I fall for the twentieth time. We're only about thirty feet from the mouth of the cave, but my knees are already bleeding. I'm trying to be a good sport, but I have zero experience spelunking, and no desire to learn. Not after this.

"Did you by any chance come across a lighter when you found that rope?"

There's a deep sigh from Alaric, but I can't see his face.

Then, suddenly, I can. There's a fire burning brightly in his…hand.

"Nachos and cheese whiz! That's--"

"Fire," Alaric says. "I made it."

"I can see that. How?" I gape.

"Everyone assumed my fae blood is weak. I felt it wasn't in my interest to do anything that might make anyone think otherwise. Why show my hand, so to speak?" Alaric smiles thinly, his eyes almost sad in the firelight.

"This is amazing," I say, coming closer to both the light and heat he's producing. "Why would you not be proud of this?"

But Alaric shakes his head. "Not when you're a young boy. And not when you accidentally set the carriage house on fire. And definitely not when your mother runs inside to save you and dies from her burns."

"Oh…" I step back, horrified. "I'm so sorry."

He closes his fist, putting the fire out and leaving us in darkness once more. "If I keep it small, I can control it. But bigger fires…" The fire wells up in his hand once more. A barely-there flicker of light, licking away at Alaric's palm but causing him no harm.

It calls to me and without thinking I reach forward and softly boop the flame. It boops me right back.

"Ouch!" I stick my burning finger into my mouth, feeling like an idiot.

"Fire is hot," Alaric tells me in his infuriatingly superior tone.

Much like Trevor and Zeus, I guess I now need to remember that Alaric has a dangerous side, too. I glance at the ball of rolling fire that he holds in his palm. I think fire wins in rock paper scissors. Like, every time.

"Don't be afraid of me, Brandee Jean," he says softly. "I will never use this against you."

"What about Trevor?" I ask, my eyes narrowing. "No one has ever seen either of you do anything supernatural. Can he do the same thing? Make fire?"

Alaric shakes his head. "I don't think so. We've always known we were enemies, so neither one of us have confided in each other."

"What could he possibly do?" I ask. "Since you're half-brothers, would he also have fire?"

"Again, I don't know for sure, but I can guess. Given his natural swimming ability and a lifelong pull toward water, I have always assumed that Trevor is an elemental, like me. But a water elemental."

"Oh," I say, remembering how easily Trevor glided in the waves. "If he's a water person thing and Zeus is a mermaid, the deck is stacked against us when the tide comes back in."

Alaric lifts his hand, lighting the tunnel a few feet ahead of us. "Not to mention, that when it does, this will all flood again. Either way, we need to push forward."

I shudder at the thought of drowning again.

"Okay," I agree. "Let's go."

12

If it wasn't for Alaric's hand full of fire, we might've tripped right over Malik.

Instead we stop at the exact same moment, surveying his body. He looks smaller in death. All the fluff has gone out of his bedraggled fur coat. He looks like a housecat that just took a bath they never asked for… one that was their last. I kneel beside him and pet his head, even though I'm pretty sure he would've hated that.

"He's still got his lion-cloth on," I say to Alaric.

"You mean loincloth," he corrects.

"No, I mean lion. He's a lion and it covered his private lion bits." Reaching down, I carefully detach his key. After a moment of hesitation, I hand it to Alaric. "Two for me. Two for you. This way if one of us goes down, whoever gets us won't get all the keys."

"Good point," he says, nodding approvingly.

I look back down at Malik, his upper lip curled into a snarl, even in death. He was so strong, so courageous, so determined to win this thing. And now, he's drowned and dead on a cave floor.

"Should we…" I trail off, already knowing the answer.

"I don't think we have time to take care of his body," Alaric says.

"Well, I think we do. Let's at least cover him in rocks. It ain't right to leave him here like this."

After a moment, Alaric nods. Silently we begin gathering rocks, which you think would be easy in a cave, but it's mostly just little pebbles scattered around us. I make a little heart shaped pebble sculpture near his head, while Alaric finds some larger stones further inside the tunnel to finish covering Malik. When we're done we stand side by side over him.

"If we survive this…what happens next?" I ask.

"No if. We will survive," Alaric corrects.

"Okay fine," I concede easily, not wanting to imagine myself under the pile of stone and pebbles that buries Malik. "But assuming neither of us wins, when we go home…what happens next?"

Alaric is quiet for a long moment. Then he sighs. "Back to our lives as they were, I suppose."

"So no fire hands?"

He chuckles softly. "No. I don't think so. Unless I'm bringing home a crown, I doubt Father would embrace my non-human side."

I lean into him. "I'll embrace your non-human side."

Alaric's arm comes around me, pulling me closer. "And what about you, Brandee Jean? Assuming the world goes back to normal once someone is in charge again, will you return to the pageant circuit?"

I think about this, trying to imagine it. First I'd have to get back into my full beauty routine. Double cleanse. Toner. Acid peel. Hydrate. Essence. Moisturizer. Makeup. And that's just my face. My whole body will need to be buffed and plucked and bronzed. Plus the mani-pedis. And my hair. Oh gods, it'll need a trim to start with. But then highlights, lowlights, a moisturizing mask combined with an intensive shampooing regimen. And exercise! Sure, I've been active here on the island, but that's not the same as concentrated toning.

And Mama, well Momzbie, will be there at my side like always. Pushing me to be better, prettier, and perkier (in all ways) than the other girls.

"We're gonna win this one," Mama would say first thing on pageant days.

We. Not you. Always we. Her and me together.

But Mama was always steering the ship. And I just went along. Even when I didn't feel like spending three hours on my nails. Or an entire evening practicing my wave and smile.

At the time it just seemed like life.

Now, though, I've seen so much more of the world. And I've been so much more. I touch the crown on my head once more, reminding myself of what I accomplished. Without Mama.

"Brandee?" Alaric nudges me. "You okay?"

"Yeah," I say, realizing that it's true. "I'm just thinking about the future and how I'm not gonna go back to how things were. First off, I'm going after Shauna. If I got super strength or not—I'm gonna find a way to get her back. And then after that, if I'm still alive, I'm gonna find a way to help people. Even if I'm not the Amazon Queen or super-powered, well look at me here. I'm a survivor. I'm—"

At the same moment we hear Trevor's voice. Alaric's hand comes over my mouth, cutting off my big speech. I give him an elbow in the side to let him know I don't need help keeping my mouth closed.

"You were sniffing around the mouth of this cave, harpy. They must be in here. Help us find them and I'll loosen those knots."

Knots? They must have captured Zahara somehow and are holding her prisoner. Which means they have her key. Crap.

There's silence for several long moments, and then louder than is comfortable, Zeus calls out, "Oh Brandee Jean, I don't wanna be mean. Come out with your big faerie, if you want to have a prayer-ee."

Alaric pushes me further into the cave. "Go," he hisses.

I stumble forward, and then take a few steps more, only to stop when I realize he's not beside me. "Alaric!" I whisper-yell.

Maybe he doesn't hear me. He turns, so he's facing the way we came in. Then, holding both hands out in front of him—he shoots.

Flame bounces from his hands, hits the ground, sizzles for a short second, and then is gone.

"Was that the plan?" I ask softly into the darkness that follows.

"Not quite." Alaric's hand latches around my arm and starts pulling me further into the cave at a pace I don't find comfortable now that we're in the pitch black once more. "Let's hope this doesn't dead end on us."

"Hope?" I throw over my shoulder. Apparently *hoping* is now the plan. But I can't argue - I don't have a better one. We're moving as fast as we can in the dark, but we're making a ton of noise, and the white flash seared onto my eyeballs from Alaric's fire-tossing means I can't see a thing. This is ridiculous. We're going to knock ourselves out cold on a cave wall, fall into an underground cavern, or just plain break our ankles and be overtaken.

"Stop," I say, grabbing Alaric's wrist. He doesn't argue, and we are both still, only listening for the next few moments.

I hear Zahara's voice, loud and rasping. "You are the last

two people who should be in charge of anything," she says. "I wouldn't let you run the slushy machine at a gas station."

There's a muffled thump and then a gasp for air. One of them just hit Zahara.

"Son of a bitch," I say under my breath. It's so dark in here, I can't see my hand in front of my face. But I can see my old friend, Shauna's face, clear as day. As if she were standing here, right now. No, not right now. Right before that awful motorcycle gang tore off with her, her voice trailing back to me on the wind.

I ran then. Instead of helping her, I ran away and I haven't stopped regretting it for a single moment since.

Here in the black of the cave, it's almost like I can smell it again - the reek of diesel and the last puff of Shauna's perfume.

"No," I say, way louder than I should. Alaric squeezes my wrist, reminding me to be quiet. But I'm not going to be. I'm not going to be little, lost, quiet Brandee Jean who just went home after her best friend was kidnapped. That Brandee Jean hadn't done anything. She'd let the bad guys win, and let who knows what happen to her friend.

It's like I was saying to Alaric before we were interrupted by Trevor and Zeus, I'm not that girl anymore. I'm somebody else now. Somebody stronger.

"Make fire," I tell Alaric, and there must be some of that strength in my voice because he does it without arguing, even though it gives up our position.

"BJ! No!" Zahara is the one that shouts when I come striding toward the trio, Zeus and Trevor flanking the harpy.

"Let her go," I say. "Now."

"Now, why would we go and do that?" Zeus asks, and one of Sora's teeth falls out of his mouth.

"Because you've already got her key," I say. "You don't need Zahara to win."

"No," Zeus shakes his head. "I don't. But I do need the ones you have. This is very simple, beauty queen. You have something I want, and I…" He pulls on the rope that binds Zahara's wings to her back, yanking her to the ground. "I have something you want."

"BJ," Zahara looks up at me, her eyes glistening in the firelight as Alaric comes closer. "I'm not even really your friend. I would have clawed your eyes out if I had to. Don't do this. Don't let one of these assholes rule the world because you'll feel bad if you leave me with them."

I ignore the harpy, my eyes locked on Zeus'. "Yes, you've got my friend, and I've got a key. But I've got something else you don't."

Clearly surprised at this tack, Zeus cocks his head. "You do? What?"

"Time," I say, pointing at his tooth, wet and glistening on the cave floor. "You're falling apart, rotting right in front of our eyes. Now I can bargain with you all day long about trading Zahara for keys, but at the end of that day, you'll be that much closer to a corpse, and I'll still have this rocking-hot body."

Beside me, Alaric clears his throat, apparently distracted at the idea of my rocking-hot body. Zeus, on the other hand, is mulling this new problem, while Trevor's eyes are on his brother's hand.

"Fire?" He asks. "Interesting."

"And," I continue, switching my focus to Trevor. "If you really want to lead the world, now would be a good time to make your case. Your master is rotting, Trevor. Or did you already put that together? Did you already figure out that if you stretch this out long enough, you'll be able to best him?"

A shadow passes over Trevor's eyes and I know that he *has* thought about it, and I already know loyalty isn't one of his strengths. Zeus knows it too; he's edging away from Trevor, turning so that his back isn't facing his former bestie.

"Trevor," he says. "You wouldn't."

It really does sound like his feelings—if Zeus has those—might be hurt.

The reflection of Alaric's fire dances in Trevor's eyes as he smiles. "You stupid old man. You never even bothered to find out who you were allying yourself with. I'm a faerie."

"Fae?" Zeus gasps. "They're born backstabbers! They'll cross someone just for a laugh."

So far as I can tell, this fits Trevor to a T. But I'm not gonna stand here and let Alaric be painted with the same brush. "Um, not all fae. Alaric's a secret faerie too…"

"Not a fan of that wording, BJ," he mutters from behind me.

I ignore him. "And he is all that is good and true and loyal and—"

"Are you trying to make me sick?" Trevor asks. "Or are you pathetically in love with my posh and proper brother? Who, by the way, will never bring you home to Father.. Don't fool yourself. Alaric sees you as nothing but an easy shag."

"He doesn't know a thing about me, Brandee," Alaric says, his voice tight with anger. The flames in his hands flare brighter.

"Easy," I say to him.

Trevor laughs while beside him, Zahara tips me a wink. Then she throws back her head and opens her mouth to emit a piercing scream.

But nothing comes out. I look at Alaric confused.

Then there's a terrible flapping from deep inside the caves. Something flies into my hair and I realize: It's a bat.

Then there's another and another. A whole freaking army of bats is fleeing the caves. I pull my shirt over my head to keep them out of my face and stumble toward Zahara.

The rope around her wrists and ankles and wings are tied tight. Stupid privileged boys and their knot tying knowledge. I'm about to try and bite through the cords when Trevor is in front of me.

"Oh BJ, your naughty bits are showing…" he tells me.

Confused, I look down and see that the keys I placed—one in each cup—in my bra are poking out. That little bastard reaches out and plucks them from my cleavage. His finger brushes my breast and I see red.

Without thinking, I punch him right in his smug face. My hand explodes with pain, but seeing his head fall back and bounce off the wall of the cave is very satisfying. Unfortunately he doesn't lose consciousness and instead scrambles back into the darkness, the bats blocking my view of him as he disappears into the shadows. There's a flash of light and I think he's dropped one of the keys, so I dive for it, getting a bat butt right in my face in the process.

But it's not a key; it's that big bowie knife that Sophia found. I grab it and cut through Zahara's binds while still swatting bats out of the way, though their frantic flight has died down.

"You saved me," Zahara says, flexing her wings.

"I wasn't going to leave you with those psychos," I tell her.

"I would have left you," she admits.

"Maybe not," I say.

"BJ, be real…" She holds a hand out and I pull her to her feet. "Since we got to this island I was out for myself but you…you tried to help Sophia. And now me. I think I was wrong about you. I would be a strong kick-ass leader, for sure. But you…"

"Ladies, we have a problem," Alaric calls.

"Are you okay?" I break away from Zahara. I was so wrapped up in saving her I didn't check on him, though I was pretty sure he could take care of himself.

"I'm uninjured," he tells me. "But...do you want the bad news or the worse news?"

I exchange a look with Zahara. "What's the bad news?" she asks.

"Well, the water is rising again."

I sigh. Great. More water. But what would be more terrible than that? "And the worse news?" I ask, dreading the answer.

"Zeus got my keys."

"What?! How could that even happen?" I demand.

"Why, did he swallow it or something?" Zahara asks. "I considered that, but didn't want to worry about losing it if I did some offensive doot slamming."

"Yeah, I found your doot slamming very offensive," I can't help but mutter.

Zahara at least has the grace to look embarrassed. "Sorry about that, BJ. In retrospect, we should've all swallowed our keys. Like you said to Zeus earlier, he's falling apart. We could've just let them travel our digestive systems while he rotted."

"I did not swallow my key," Alaric jumps into the conversation. "And I rather resent your insinuation that Zeus was able to get my key because I shat myself."

I can't help but giggle at this. "It's so cute. You even say shit fancy."

"Ugh, stop flirting," Zahara says with an eye roll. "So then how did the big Z get your keys?"

He reached up my shirt. I couldn't get the flames out of my hands to stop him, so I just stood there while he used this little Swiss Army knife and cut them away." Alaric pulls up his shirt to reveal the cut ropes dangling from his equally cut chest.

"Well, while Zeus was feeling you up, Trevor was patting

me down. If I get my super strength back, I'm gonna break his fingers." The little pervert.

"We have to get back to the statue," Zahara says.

"We can't let Zeus win," I add.

"Alaric, light the way," I order. "Zahara, once we get out there I need you to fly us to that statue...can you hold both of us?"

"For a short distance, yes." She nods.

"Good. When we get there it's going to be a fight. No matter which of us goes down, we do not let Zeus or Trevor win, agreed?"

"Absolutely," Zahara says.

I look to Alaric, eyebrows raised.

"We will not let them win," he agrees.

"Let's go!" I clap my hands and as Alaric goes past me with his light he whispers something that gives me goosebumps.

"Brandee, you've inspired me to rethink my future plans. You're right, after everything here, we can't go back to the way things were."

"So you're embracing your fae side?"

"No, I'd like to embrace my BJ side." He stops. Frowns. "That doesn't sound right. I want to embrace you. That is...I'd love to have you meet my family."

13

Zahara lands us in the valley. Zeus and Trevor are already there, fiddling with the keys.

"You're too late, brother," Trevor yells. His nose is crooked and I feel wickedly satisfied that I've broken it. "The power is..." He pauses, darting a glance sideways. "Zeus."

Alaric tries again to throw a fireball but it goes wide and lands in the rising tide. The water is coming over the rim of the canyon again, but not as fast as it was earlier. It's like the gods want to see how this plays out.

Trevor grins and gathers up a ball of water that he throws back. It knocks Alaric on his ass. Zeus already has all but one of the keys in place, all of them turned in their locks. There's only one left, and my heart sinks at the sight. We all resolved to be a team and not let Zeus win, but right now it feels like we just said empty words in that cave.

"What can we do?" Zahara asks.

I shake my head. What *can* we do?

"Give me the diamond one, assistant," Zeus calls over his shoulder. Trevor hands it to him reluctantly, keeping an eye on the three of us as he does. Zahara shoots to the sky, dividing his attention, but it's too late.With the last key in place the stone base rumbles and the front swings open. I creep closer to get a better look. Inside is a golden chest, an unearthly glow emanating from it.

Zeus cackles, another flap of skin falling from his face. "That's it, boy. It contains all my power. I can feel it pulsing. It wants to come back to me."

"But the inscription…" Trevor trails off. "Earlier you said-_"

"Yes, the puzzle. *Those who seek shall not find. Those who find shall not seek.*" Zeus coughs up a squirming mess of maggots and spits them on the ground. "It's hogwash. A red herring to turn away those of lesser courage."

"It's not," I shout out. Trying to distract them, inching closer. "It's obvious what it means."

"It is?" Zeus asks, like he's entertaining the whims of a child. His hands are on the chest, ready to flip it open. But he wants to toy with me too. He's already won. Now he just wants to make sure we all know it.

"If you want the power, you can't have it. That's what it means," I hazard. But it makes perfect sense.

"I'll open it for you!" Trevor offers, stepping forward. "What if it's a trap? I don't want to be king of the gods. All I want is to serve you."

"Liar," Alaric shouts.

Zahara drops back to the ground. "Don't trust him!" she shouts.

"I don't want it!" Trevor insists. "I'll open the chest and give the power to you."

Zeus doesn't look convinced. Then Trevor adds, "Oh great and powerful king."

Zeus grins, his head more skull than skin. "Do it, boy."

Trevor goes forward, takes a deep breath, and opens the

chest. Alaric, Zahara, and I all freeze, expecting the worst. Trevor's idea about it being booby-trapped wasn't a bad one. I'm ready for flying arrows, a zombie, or an explosion.

But all I hear is the sound of lapping water as the tide rushes toward us once more, the canyon beginning to fill again, licking at my ankles.

"Well?" Zeus demands as he takes a step toward Trevor.

"It's a sword," Trevor reports.

"Give it to me," Zeus says, holding out a hand. He pauses, snatching his hand back. "Actually, pick up the chest and tell me to take the sword. And then I'll say, 'Oh no, I'm not worthy of it. I messed up last time. I don't deserve a do-over.' And then you'll say, 'No, Zeus, only you can handle this power. Only you can be king of the gods. It would be selfish of you to refuse.' We'll go back and forth like that a few times and then finally, I'll take it. You got that?"

Zahara shakes her head. "Those are just words, old man. The gods will know what's in your heart. Brandee's right. If you want that sword, you can't have it. And you can be sure they will stop you."

"Sure, sure. Great plan," Trevor says, reaching down into the chest. Anyone with eyes can see he's intending to take the sword for himself, but Zeus seems to still believe Trevor is on his side. Maybe thousands of years of having everyone suck up to you does that to someone.

"Brother, don't," Alaric says softly. "If Brandee is correct..."

"That white trash, bargain basement beauty queen?" he scoffs. "I might take her advice on discount panty hose, but not much else."

I seethe. "You are going to regret..."

He reaches for the sword. "I regret nothing," he says as he grabs the hilt, pulling it free. It gleams brightly, lit with supernatural power.

He holds it above his head. "I feel...so..." He grins. "Powerful." His skin begins to glow, the light from the sword draining into his body. "It's rushing through me. I am the king of the gods." He's bright white now, like the hottest burning flame. I put my hand up to shield my eyes and there is a loud sound like the bang of an explosion.

Trevor disappears like a popped balloon. The sword falls back into the golden chest, which slams shut with a clang.

Alaric's fists clench. "That idiotic, selfish, dastardly..." But there is pain on his face. He loved his brother, even if he was a little weasel.

"What...?" Zeus looks shocked. "I don't understand."

"He was never going to give you the power," I tell him. "He wanted it for himself."

"Then who can claim it?" he asks. "We all want to win."

I shake my head. I *did* want to win. I wanted the crown and the glory. I wanted to win because ever since I was a little girl and Mama entered me in Miss Turnpike Toddler she had ingrained in me that *need* to win. To beat everyone else. To grab the crown.

But it was never enough. There was always another contest. Another crown.

I had to prove myself over and over again.

Being Amazon Queen would be just like that.

But worse.

Athena would definitely be up my ass 24/7. And I'm pretty sure I'd be immortal too, so it would basically never end.

At least in the pageant world I knew that eventually I'd age out.

After talking with Alaric about the future, I realized I don't want to do pageants anymore. I want to live my own life. But how could I do that if I was in charge of literally everything? I joined the prom committee at school last year, 'cause Mama figured it'd give me the inside track on being crowned Queen. It seemed like it would be fun, but I was wrong. Instead we spent four weeks arguing over whether gold and silver or gold and black were a more elegant color duo. It really soured me on the whole idea of being in charge of anything. But unless you're a dictator then committees are kinda like the thing you have to do all the time. And I definitely don't want to be a dictator.

I don't want all the bullshit that goes with being in charge. I just want to live a normal life. Have a boyfriend. Maybe meet my boyfriend's parents in their fancy English mansion. Get some hobbies. Maybe visit a beach in a place where I'm not fighting for my life.

"Go ahead, give it a shot," Zahara tells Zeus. "I'm sure you're worthy...I mean, it was your power originally, so..."

Zeus shakes his rotting head. "Nice try, harpy. I'm going to have to think about this a little longer. Maybe if I kill the rest of you I'll win by default."

Alaric, shoulders bowed, says, "I'll go next. I want to win but...maybe it *is* about worthiness. Trevor was always selfish. He would have been a terrible leader. I'd be a fair king."

I stick my tongue out and spray Alaric with some good old Wisconsin raspberries. "That is the dumbest thing I've ever heard."

Of course he gets all stiff and offended. It's possible nobody has ever called him dumb before. Or sprayed spit in his face. I'm pretty sure the British have better manners than Midwesterners, on principle.

"She's right," Zahara says. "Dying isn't noble. And your 'fair king' crap is a load of doot too."

"I see," he says, in a tone that makes it clear the only thing he's seeing right now is red.

Zeus cackles. "Or maybe I don't have to kill you. Maybe you'll kill each other." He grins. "I'd love to see some girl on girl action first. And then whoever survives can take on the boy. Oooh, ooh, ooh." His eyes light up and for a moment I get a small sense of what he once was, but even that is unattractive. "Let's make it even more interesting. You all strip down and wrestle in the mud."

"Did all this power corrupt you?" Alaric asks Zeus as he studies him with disdain. "Or were you always this way?"

Zeus is obviously confused by the question. "What way?"

"Gross," Zahara and I answer simultaneously.

"How dare you," Zeus blusters. "I'm king of the gods and once I regain my power, things will go back the way they're supposed to be."

I roll my eyes. "If any of us win, we'll put the world back together and try to stop all the chaos and fighting."

"Stop the chaos!?" Zeus throws his head back and laughs. "My dear dear girl. We won't stop it. We'll redirect it. That's how we keep the world intact, by controlling the fighting. People need something to be mad at. In the past we've just let them be mad at each other. Now that our worlds have collided, people have united against the paranormal. It's World War III."

I look to Alaric and Zahara who seem less stunned than me. "I don't understand," I say. "The gods are in on the fighting? You have the power to stop all this, but you don't?"

"Of course! Don't act so shocked." Zeus winks at me like we're on the same side and if my stomach wasn't empty I probably would throw up in my mouth. "The gods have been around for a long, long time. We've seen it all, and we get bored easily. Not so long ago, the monsters and paranormals were our playthings—ask your dragon mentor Edie about it sometime. We watch. We direct. We cheer on our faithful soldiers. Sometimes we eat popcorn. Oh, and we educate, of course, because it's best to start them young. So all the good-looking creatures, you know, the witches, the vamps, the shifters—they were on our side. While the uglies, like her—" He points a finger Zahara's way. "She's a monster, of course."

I stare at Zahara, horrified. "She's not a monster!" I cry.

"Technically, I am," she says. "Everything he's saying is awful, but it's true. The gods pitted paranormals against monsters in the magical world for a long time. And it sounds like now there's whole new production. People vs Paranormals part II, Bigger, Better, Deader—with the biggest god of all as the director."

I shake my head. "I wouldn't do that. If I won this thing, I'd create peace on Earth."

Alaric shakes his head. "Wow, you went full on beauty queen there."

"I would!" I insist, stamping my foot.

Zeus shrugs. "Maybe for the first few thousand years, but trust me. You'll get bored."

Zahara takes a step toward Zeus. The sort of movement that is full of intent. He shrinks back. "Wait, what are you doing?"

Zahara smiles. "I'm going to give Sora the burial at sea that he deserved and that is long overdue." Her wings spread out and suddenly she's on top of Zeus, her claws sinking into his soft flesh.

"No! Harpy scum!" He tries to slap at her with his remaining hand and in his frenzy, it flies off, landing at my feet. His eyes lock with mine. "Please, beautiful girl, help me. When I re-open Mount Olympus Academy, you'll be my top student—AUGH!"

Zahara lifts into the sky taking Zeus with her.

"Guess my ugly face is going to be the last thing you see," she says.

Zeus' undead hand reaches for my boot and with a shriek, I scramble backwards. Alaric leaps forward and stomps it.

There's a soft "pooft" sound and whatever life was in it leaks out...along with some puss. The fingers twitch in the sand.

"Ew," I say. "I could've done that, but I'm really glad that mess isn't on the bottom of my shoe."

He gives a little bow. "It's not quite as elegant as using a cape to cover a puddle, but it will have to do."

"Does this mean you're done being mad at me for calling your idea dumb?" I give my best "you can't stay mad at little "ole me" smile.

He melts like I'm the one who can make fire. "You may want to consider taking some courses in diplomacy should you win the crown. Because while you may have had a point, calling one names and spraying spittle at them is not the best way to get them across."

I put my hands on my hips. "Well if you win, maybe you'll need classes in saying stuff simpler and with less words. Like, you coulda just said, 'BJ, you were totally right, but the delivery sucked.'"

"I would not agree that you were totally right—"

I interrupt Alaric as a brilliant idea occurs to me. "What if we just co-rule? We'd be such a good team!"

"Um, excuse me?" Zahara lands between us. "I'm gone for two seconds, and you two are already cutting me out of the deal-making?"

"No, of course not," Alaric holds his hands out toward Zahara in an appeasing sort of way. "You took care of a distasteful but necessary task and we appreciate it."

I shake my head. "Too many words again. All you gotta say is, 'Girl, I owe you a manicure for getting all that gross Zeus goop on your talons.'" I turn to her. "So?"

"Well, I flew out over the ocean and then started ripping parts off of him, one by one. His head I fed to a nearby shark. Poor creature. But Zeus should be ocean poop very soon."

I hesitate a minute, expecting to feel remorse. Or at least a shred of sadness for that desperate wreck of a former god. But instead I remember him killing Rada. And Sophia.

"Good riddance." I say. "Also, ick. Think we owe you a pedi to go with that mani."

Zahara smiles. "I may take you up on that. Especially since I think we might have some time to kill. That is if you both agree to my suggestion."

"Spill," I demand.

"They want us to go all Hunger Games on each other, but maybe the gods forgot how that movie ended."

"Actually, it was a book first," Alaric interrupts.

Zahara and I both just look at him. I mean, really.

He clears his throat. "Continue."

"At the end, the girl and her boy-toy refuse to kill each other and basically force the contest makers to let them split the win."

"I love it," I squeal. "So we just wait them out, right? And in the meantime, we can re-enact a scene from another movie. The makeover scene from The Breakfast Club." Whipping the mascara out from where it's been nestled between my breasts, I take a step toward Zahara. "I'm gonna Molly Ringwald you."

"I'll pass," Zahara jumps back. But I'm not letting her get away that easily.

Or maybe I am. Alaric steps between us. "You left out an important part."

Zahara and I exchange another look. Sure Alaric is hunky and handsome and honorable. It's why I'm continuously drawn to him, even when sometimes he acts like the most pretentious know-it-all to ever walk the earth.

"Please, Alaric, mansplain Hunger Games to us," Zahara says in a deadpan voice.

"I'm not mansplaining—" Clearly exasperated, he stops. "Bollocks. Maybe I am mansplaining. Regardless, this bit is rather important. The two characters threaten to kill themselves. They risk their own lives for the win."

"Oooh," Zahara nods. "Okay, the mansplainer has a point. And I like it. Especially since your addendum to my plan stops this whole breakfast makeover thing."

I sigh. "You guys have lost me."

"We're all going to grab the sword at once," Alaric explains.

"And just hope we don't go kablooey?" I ask.

Zahara shrugs. "Got a better idea? We can wait for the tide to come in again, but my bet is the gods will find something new to throw at us until one of us gets fed up enough to claim the sword. At least if we all poof out of existence, it won't be our problem anymore."

I'm not really loving this new twist on the plan.

"Let's pinky-swear that we'll share the powers. We'll vote and act as one when necessary so the full power of Zeus will still exist in the world."

"I like it," Alaric says. "Although I'm not sure I know exactly how one pinky swears."

"Yeah," Zahara adds. "Especially when I don't have any pinkies."

"Okay, everyone just put their hand or talon or whatever in," I say.

I place my hand palm down. Alaric's big warm one falls softly on mine. And then Zahara's sharp talon tops us both. "I swear to share the power of Zeus. Majority vote will determine our actions when we disagree."

Alaric nods at Zahara. His shoulders go back so he's standing even stiffer than usual. I think this is his official oath swearing stance. "I swear to share the powers of Zeus and to wield the powers given to me fairly and with equal say to the two women before me."

Finally, it's my turn. I shuffle my feet so I'm in the right stance and then announce, "I swear to share the powers of Zeus since having one dude be king of all the gods was obviously not a super great idea. We're all taught from a very young age, like even before kindergarten, that we should share. That sharing is good. Maybe Zeus never learned this lesson. He kept all the power for himself and in the end, it killed him. Well, actually his bastard daughter killed him, which brings up another good lesson about keeping it in your pants. And if you can't do that, at least keep track of your offspring. No one likes a deadbeat daddy. In conclusion, Zeus was a turd-burger. I promise we will do like way way better." I pause. Flash my pearly whites. And then finish with a classic, "Thank you for your time."

"Oh gods," Zahara says softly as we pull apart. "I hope I don't regret this."

"Let's hope we live to regret this," Alaric says. "We don't know if we'll be alive after touching that sword."

He's right, I realize. We're all thinking forward to a future that might not exist. This island might be the end for us.

With that in mind, I throw myself at Alaric. I stand on my tippy toes and give him a kiss on his chin. "Despite your arrogance and your stubbornness and your infernal manners, I really like you, Alaric."

He moves his head down and I push my lips to his.

"One last snorg," I say. "Just in case."

"Snog," he corrects me gently. "We say snog."

I knew it was something gross like that. Although I don't say that to Alaric. Instead, I keep my lips on his and then my tongue too, trying to tell him that whatever else happens, we'll always have this island. We pull apart

"What, no snog for me?" Zahara asks.

Alaric blushes. "I prefer to only snog with one girl at a time."

"Your loss," Zahara says with a mischievous smile.

Then there's no more putting it off. We approach the chest together. In sync we each reach out a hand and pull the lid open. Inside is the golden sword, glimmering from within.

"Ready?" Alaric asks.

Zahara and I both nod.

"On the count of three," he says.

"Why do you get to count?" Zahara asks.

"Shouldn't it be a countdown? It feels more momentous, doesn't it?" I add.

Alaric sighs. "Fine. We'll countdown together. Ready?"

"From ten," I say, even though I know the other two are ready to murder me. "If these are our last moments, I'd rather have ten than three."

"Ten then," Zahara agrees between clenched teeth.

"On one or after one?"

"BJ!" Alaric sighs in frustration.

"It's an important distinction!"

"One then touch," Zahara says.

"Okay, one then touch." I repeat. I really, really don't want to mess this up.

Together we count. "10, 9, 8, 7, 6, 5, 4, 3, 2, 1…"

Our hands hover over the sword and then all at once we grab for the hilt.

My fingers close around cold metal and then, as one, we're lifting it up.

I feel the power emanating through me and I know that I'm glowing as white hot as Alaric and Zahara beside me. Alaric's hand overlaps mine and Zahara's claw might rip off my thumb, but right now it doesn't matter. Pressure builds in my chest, coursing through me.

I can feel the strength I'd had before returning, along with a pulsing warmth that must be the healing power Rada had inherited. I feel amazing! Underneath that, I can feel them all.

Zahara's knowledge, Constantine's fertility, Trevor's shape-shifting, Alaric's teleportation, and Sora's charm. It's too much. No one should have all these gifts. Even split among the three of us... No wonder Trevor exploded.

I close my eyes, ready to pop like a balloon, but it never comes.

When I open them I am still in the valley. Alaric and Zahara gape back at me, the sword raised over our heads.

We're still alive.

And I think we just became immortal.

14

I just won the biggest prize in history, and all I want to do is cry. But there's no time. When I open my eyes again, all three of us are back on the stage at Amazon Academy.

We are all still holding the sword overhead. Actually, now it's swords. Plural. We each have one. It seems like the original one somehow duplicated itself...with some minor adjustments. Alaric's is silver, all straight lines and some scrollwork on the hilt that screams wealth and privilege. Zahara's is black and ragged, deadly beautiful. Mine is gold, and gleams brighter than any crown I've ever worn. The hilt is inlaid with diamonds and a single red ruby. I wonder if these are our official swords for all time or if we can trade depending on what we're wearing, current trends, etc.

And this probably isn't the greatest time to ask; as soon as Hades sees what we've done—and that his brother didn't make it back—his face turns into a mask of anger.

"Undead! Attack!" He screams, and all the zombies who had been standing like sentinels in the aisles of the auditorium rush the stage and dive into the audience as well, teeth snapping, ragged nails clawing.

Without even discussing it, the three of us spin so our backs are to one another and start swinging our swords. But even as zombies fall, more take their place.

Around me I can see Amazons, Athena, Artemis, and a few other gods fighting as well.

But there's no sign of my mom. I hope nobody accidentally cuts her down.

"Um, we're gods now, so maybe we should do something more than just chop at zombies with our swords," Zahara says, her breath catching in her throat as she swings. A decapitated head flies off into the audience, eyes wide with surprise as it rolls into the back rows..

"If you're chopping, you're really not handling your sword correctly," Alaric says.

"You know what, Alaric?" Zahara sounds more than a little pissed off. "I have my super intelligence back, so I don't really need you explaining the correct positioning for swordplay. I could give you the entire history of the sword dating back to 1600 BC."

"You're super smart again?" I jump in before Zahara and Alaric start using their swords on each other. "I guess that means I'm super strong. And Alaric, you can probably teleport. I wonder what else we got? It kinda feels a little like Christmas morning, doesn't it?"

"Christmas morning with zombies," Alaric agrees, taking one out at the knees. It crumples, but pulls what's left of its body to the edge of the stage, still snapping at the Amazon's ankles. One of them glances down briefly, squashes its head with her heel, and jumps back into the melee.

"I can't feel anything new," Zahara says. "And I'm usually very in touch with my body. The only thing I sense are some menstrual cramps."

"Um, guys," I say with a laugh. "I've got this almost gassy feeling and I think—" A boom of thunder shakes the ground around us. It's followed by a bolt of lightning that leaves a smoking blackened crater in the ground where at least a dozen zombies had been.

"BJ was that you?" Alaric asks.

"Yeah it was!" I cry out. "How cool was that?"

"Can you do it again?" Zahara asks. "Just don't hit us or anyone who isn't a zombie."

"It would help to have a higher vantage point," I say.

In an instant we're at the top of a nearby tower, overlooking the zombie outbreak below.

"Nice," I say to Alaric as I turn to him with a smile. The smile freezes and then slides away. "Gooble gok," I say, pointing at Alaric, having lost any control I ever had over the English language.

Zahara looks as well, but seems less struck than me. "Okay, well, Alaric clearly got beauty. Nice improvement to your Brit geek look."

I spin on Zahara. "How dare you! Alaric was a prize hunk of UK beefsteak. And now he's…" I dart a glance at Alaric, but quickly have to look away again. He's so gorgeous it almost hurts my eyes. And it totally fries my brain. I try just looking at his feet, but even those are beautiful beyond anything I've ever seen. It's taking all my super strength to keep from jumping his bones.

This is gonna be a problem for us working together. And for our relationship, if we intend to do anything other than snorg. Snob. Snort. Snickle. Yep, I've lost English.

But first—the zombies.

"Okay, I'm gonna fry these undead uglies. But I don't know if that's enough to stop them," I say.

"It's not," Zahara replies. "According to my calculations Hades raised all the dead. Anybody that still has enough musculature to fight has been risen and sent to attack. At this rate, they'll keep coming for the next six months."

"Six months!" I cry.

"Unless," Alaric adds in. "Hades tells them to stop."

"Okay, so teleport Hades' ass over here," I say.

"Actually, I have a better idea." Alaric smiles and I quickly look away before I get dazzled again. "I'll become Hades." And with that he shape-shifts into Hades.

"Seriously!? You got shifting?" Zahara throws her arms up. "If Alaric has beauty, shifting and teleportation. BJ has lightning, thunder, and strength. What does that leave for me?"

"Flying?" I suggest.

"I can already fly!"

I think hard about flying, but nothing happens. "Well, I still can't."

"Me neither," Alaric adds. "Sorry, Zahara."

"Unbelievable," she mutters.

"You probably got healing," I tell Zahara. "And that's one of the best ones."

She brightens for a moment but then frowns again. "If I had healing, I wouldn't have period cramps, which are getting worse by the way." Zahara's face changes suddenly. "Oh shit! I got virility!"

"Oh no, Zahara! That sucks," I say, although really I'm thinking 'thank the gods it wasn't me.' Then I remember Constantine's constant hard on and half regret that Alaric didn't get it.

"Wait," Zahara says. "If I concentrate, the cramps go away. Maybe I did get healing after all!"

"Or perhaps we all received a portion of healing power," Alaric suggests. Testing his theory, he touches a finger to the edge of his sword. Blood immediately wells up.

"Alaric, how can you do that to your beautiful perfect

thumb!" Even as I say this, though, his skin starts to close up again.

"Great, we're all immortal and super healers. Now let me test out my new and improved flying powers." Zahara grabs Alaric from behind and flaps up into the air. "Come on Hades, I'll fly you out over the zombies and you can tell them to be dead again."

I watch as Zahara flies easily despite Alaric's extra weight. As they reach the front of the wave, they dip lower and Alaric calls out, "Zombies, return to your graves! Rest your weary bones until I need to call upon you once more!"

It's the worst impersonation of Hades ever. Alaric definitely doesn't have his brother's natural gift for imitation. And yet, the zombies pause to stare up at him. And when he repeats the message, they start to turn back the way they came.

"My gods, it's working," I say softly.

"BJ, your new boyfriend looks a lot like my new boyfriend."

I spin to find a woman who looks like a cheap stripper in front of me. She's got huge knockers, way too much glittery blue eye-shadow, and perfectly placed false eyelashes.

"Mama?" I ask.

"Yes, baby, it's me!" She throws her arms around me for a hug and then quickly pulls away. "Well, what do you think?" She runs her hands down her new body. "Hades upgraded me. My old body was making him literally nauseous and then he came across this one. Poor girl overdosed and then was put in cold storage at the morgue to await ID'ing. She'd been chilling out there since the whole world went kablooey."

"That's great, Mama," I force myself to say. It feels like old times. Mama with a shitty new boyfriend who everyone can see is terrible, but she thinks is a catch. At least she looks great. "And you finally got those double D's you always wanted!"

"Can you believe it?" Mama grins and then bounces a little so I can see the girls in action. "There's still some pink scar tissue, so I think it was a fairly recent boob job. I'm so perky, I gotta get some tube tops to really show these off. Hades promised we'd go shopping after, well never mind. How are *you* doing, sweetie?"

"Well, I'm good. I won the contest."

Mama makes a face. "You kinda won. Hades says you split it."

I sigh. "Mama, if you already knew, then why did you ask?"

"Baby, I'm proud of you. That's why I'm here. Hades and I are going to hit the road—he's got big plans and I'm gonna help him. But I had to see you first and tell you how proud I am."

Mama reaches for me again, pulling me in for another hug. Mama prefers micro-hugs. A quick squeeze and then it's over. I'm a god now, though. A god with super strength. So I just hold onto her. Her new breasts are hard against my chest, without any give or softness. But I don't let go. "Mama, I missed you," I tell her.

"I missed you too," she says as I finally let her pull away. She reaches a hand out and smooths a piece of my hair back. "All that sun has bleached out your hair," she tsks softly. "We'll have to do a spa day together when my trip with Hades is over."

I frown. "What is this trip?"

"I've actually gotta skadoodle right now. Hades is waiting and once a man gives you a new body, he tends to think that he owns it."

"But, Mama, I've barely seen you! And by the way, your

new boyfriend just tried to kill everyone with a horde of zombies."

"Oh sweetheart, you don't need me. You've got the powers of a god now. And Hades, well... What's that one Pearl Jam song? *Can't Find A Better Man?*" She smiles and there's lipstick on her teeth. I know she would hate that, but I don't tell her it's there. I'm too mad. And hurt. It feels like the last time she left me. When she took that bottle of pills and checked out. She used the same, 'you've got super powers, you don't need me' excuse then, too. As if being strong means a girl doesn't need her mom.

"Mama, please, don't go," I say, my voice cracking as I grab for her hand.

"BJ!" Mama pulls her hand away. "Don't scuff up my new body! It's not like perfect specimens are just waiting in coolers all over the world. I got lucky this time." She pats my cheek. "And now I gotta make sure Hades gets lucky too, if you know what I mean." With that she disappears down the winding staircase.

"Mama!" I call after her, even though I know she won't stop or even turn around. I've always been Mama's number one...until a new man comes around. Sure, she never let any of them beat me up or feel me up, but that's cold comfort when I'm in an empty house alone eating canned soup while she and her new beau are hitting the bars. I told Mama I hated being home alone and she'd just tell me to suck it up and toughen up. I begged her not to leave me in the apocalypse and I got the same speech.

Just once, I wish she truly would make me her number one and not her number one for right now.

"Bye, Mama," I say. But she doesn't even look back.

15

———

Athena is so pleased that an Amazon has become one of the leaders of the gods that she offers to help me with, well, everything. The Amazons are at my disposal and she has a list of all the things I have to do first. She's even created a place for me to reign, a temple of my own to dispatch underlings and make proclamations.

I'm grateful for her help, but it's not me. I sit on a golden throne in a room without a floor. Instead clouds carpet the ground...soft and beautiful. Lightning bolts decorate the walls. It's very, very Zeus.

Also, it was only made for one god. Not three. It's weird to sit on a throne while Alaric and Zahara are next to me on metal folding chairs. They don't look too happy about it, either. But I'm still teary-eyed over Mama picking a man over me (again). I don't feel like being Athena's favorite is going to sit well with the other two, but my mind—and heart —are still reeling. I'll sort it out with them later.

We were given a little time to clean up after Alaric ordered the zombies away, but then our break was over. Athena came marching in along with a whole bunch of advisors, and my new Amazon guard. Apparently, they're like the Amazon equivalent of the Secret Service, which I guess makes me the president.

It's weird.

Athena begins to quickly run down all the threats currently facing the world. First all the rogue gods who've been running wild and doing what they want. We gotta stop that nonsense, but the gods are, of course, going to question our authority, especially since we split Zeus' powers three ways. They're not used to that, and are going to push back, Athena warns us with a scowl. I know she's not happy with me for choosing to split the powers, but I can't find the energy to care about her feelings right now. I've got a world to run.

The humans are not accepting the presence of paranormals on their planet very well, and in true human fashion, they've been doing everything they can to fight them. Apparently silver bullets are in high demand and garlic is now a cash crop. Normally regular people wouldn't stand a chance against all the supernaturals, but there's enough in-fighting on the paranormal side for the humans to have something of an advantage, Athena explains.

"Divide and conquer," Alaris says under his breath.

Apparently all the lesser supernatural creatures have been grappling for power. The fae and vampires are engaged in a full-out war against one another, with the Midwest as their main battlefield. Shifters have moved into packs, some of them meant just to protect themselves with safety in numbers, but others are much more destructive—fatalities among humans that stand against them are high. Also, a group of evil witches and warlocks have seized several Canadian cities. Athena rolls her eyes at that last one. "They swear maple syrup has mystical powers beyond anything on the planet, but no one really believes that."

"However," Athena finishes, "our biggest threat at the moment is incredible seismic activity that is supernatural in origin."

With a wave of her hand a globe shimmers in the air before us and slowly rotates. Several little dots light up on it, which I presume are the places in question.

But it's not the most important thing to me. "How do I heal my mother?" I blurt out. "My mama has a new body, but she's gonna start rotting again eventually!"

"Um, BJ, not really the time," Zahara says.

"Brandee Jean, I thought you realized," Athena says with a frown. "Hades split once he realized his brother wasn't going to be running the show anymore, and your mother chose to go with him."

"Hades promised her a new pair of boobies," I tell Athena. "And he delivered. She didn't have options. Her body was falling apart."

"I offered her the chance to take a spirit form and stay by your side for all eternity," Athena counters. "She turned me down flat."

My heart sinks and tears threaten. I mean, sure, that is a killer rack Hades found for Mama, but she didn't even consider getting spiritual to stay with her daughter?

Still I don't want all these people thinking bad of Mama. "Mama also mentioned that Hades promised her a shopping trip and I know for a fact that it's been her lifelong dream to take advantage of Tata's Tops year-round five tube tops for twenty bucks deal." I sniffle, suddenly missing Mama worse than ever even though I just saw her a little bit ago. "She always said if she ever got her boobs done, she'd be their best customer ever."

"Excuse me," Alaric politely interrupts. I look his way, but once again his unbearable hotness is more than I can take. I don't want to be turned on when I'm sad about Mama betraying me. "One of the hot spots on your globe just grew brighter." Squinting, he stands and walks closer. "It appears to be in…Wisconsin."

I look at the map. "That's right by my home," I say. "How could that be a target, unless…not to be self-centered, but is someone trying to get at me?"

Alaric comes over and pulls me tight against his chest. I breathe in and realize that even his smell is more attractive than before. "Let's go to Wisconsin. We'll stop whatever is happening there."

"And find Shauna too?" I sniffle.

"Wait. Who the heck is Shauna?" Zahara demands.

Athena steps forward. "Hold on. We have advisors here to help you make the best decision—"

"No way," Zahara shakes her head. "We've got the power and all these advisors just want a piece of it. That's not happening. We'll figure this out ourselves. That's what we pledged to each other on the island, and that's what we're sticking to." She looks to me and Alaric. "Right?"

I look at the advisors and remember the prom committee. "Yeah, let's skip the advisors."

"Agreed," Alaric says.

"Great." Zahara nods while Athena sputters. "Everyone who's going to Wisconsin, raise your hand." My hand goes up along with my two Amazon guards. "Nope. Nuh-uh. Not on this mission," Zahara tells the warriors and she pushes their arms back down. This takes a while since the Amazons aren't easily cowed, but eventually Zahara wins. "We're ready for takeoff, Alaric."

He gulps. "Right. A multi-person trip halfway around the globe without any practice or any idea of what the place I'm aiming for looks like can't possibly end in disaster."

I pat his arm and then rub it and then squeeze it and am just about to sink my teeth into it just to give him a taste, when I remember what I was going to say. "Aim for a cartoon pig head wearing a white hat."

"A pig?" Alaric asks.

"Cartoon pig," I correct. "Kinda like Porky Pig."

"Of course. That is actually rather how I've always imagined much of the States."

And with those words, we disappear.

16

I am standing in the parking lot of the Piggly Wiggly where this all started.

But this time, Alaric and Zahara are at my side. I squeal. "Home sweet home," I say.

Alaric looks around. "Charming," he says to me in a tone which means he thinks it's anything but.

"Look, I know it's a shithole, but it's *my* shithole." I tell him, hands on hips.

"No," he says hastily. "It's great...I love the..." He looks around. "Pikes of rotting corpses."

Well, that's new. Decorating the parking lot are about ten bodies on spears. They're in various states of decomposition. Each wears a leather vest. "What the shit happened here?" I ask.

"We gotta check in the store. My friend Carl ran it." I grimace, hoping he's not on a pike behind the counter.

The automatic door slides open for me as I walk in, which normally wouldn't be an amazing feat, but that door has been busted for six months.

Carl looks up from behind the counter in amazement.

"Brandee Jean?" he asks, pushing his glasses up his nose. "Is that really you?"

"Yes!" I look around. Everything seems fine. Just the same as the last time I was in.

"Back so soon? Didn't expect you until next month."

"Soon?" I repeat, bewildered. It feels like a million years since I was whisked away to Amazon Academy. "How long were we competing?" I ask my friends.

"A week, I think," Zahara says. "Though I would guess the island exists outside of the space time continuum."

"You were in here ten days ago," Carl tells me. "I know because that's when the Devil Wings decided this was their turf. They've killed a Pink Pussy every day since then to scare them away. But they aren't exactly pushovers, those Pussies."

"Excuse me," Alaric asks, eyebrows raised. "Pink Pussy?"

Carl focuses on him for the first time. "You are…" Carl eyes him up and down, then clears his throat. "A handsome boy."

"The Pink Pussies are a motorcycle gang," I explain. "The Devil Wings too. All the Motorcycle clubs got super hard core around here after, well, you know."

"Who's your friend?" Carl asks, still eye-humping Alaric. "I have never wanted to have sex with a man before but…"

I step in front of his line of vision. Carl shakes his head. "Did I really say that? I don't know what came over me."

"It's a god thing," I explain. "My friend Alaric here is extra beautiful, and Zahara is super smart."

"Also ovulating," she says, giving Carl a smile and a wink.

"And I got a few powers as well…strength, healing, lightning." I stop, realizing that he's going to have a million questions.

"Oh," Carl nods, unfazed. "That makes sense about the door working, then."

I laugh. "Yeah...I guess I'm a one-woman electric generator."

Carl nods again like this isn't all that odd, either. And I guess it probably isn't. When Zeus died we were all thrown into a world where vampires and shifters and monsters lived alongside each other with the humans, breaking down the magical barriers between our worlds and running amok.

"If you became a god and got powers, why did you ever come back to Wisconsin?" Carl asks.

"This magic globe thingy showed that Wisconsin might be going kablooey soon from some seismic activity, so we're here to…" I frown, realizing our plan didn't really go beyond 'visit Wisconsin.' "Well, we'll just be here if anything bad happens."

"Sorta like superpowered firefighters?" Carl asks.

"Dear gods, no." Alaric says. "My family would be horrified if I joined the fire brigade…"

"But you would look so hot in the uniform," I say, unable to keep from rubbing my hands on his chest.

"He really would," Carl agrees.

"We're going to sort the world out," Zahara says, stepping between Carl and Alaric. "We're still working out the how, but we'll figure it out."

"Totally," I agree. "And in the meantime, I gotta set something right that I did wrong a long time ago."

Carl nods. "BJ, it's okay. My dad and I knew you distracted us so your mom could steal makeup."

"Wait. What?" I am shocked. I mean, sure, Mama would sometimes treat herself to some discounted merch at the big department stores, but only because they're owned by big evil corporations. It's like she always said, "Stealing from crooks isn't a crime, it's an act of heroism." But I never knew Mama was stealing from our friends and neighbors too. And making me her unknowing accomplice.

"Carl, I had no idea and I'm so sorry. Mama was...well, she probably only did it once or twice, right?"

"Oh no," Carl shakes his head. "We could never catch her in the act, but going from inventory, it was a pretty regular occurrence, just about every time she came in. Probably for the best we could never pin her down. Dad always used to say he didn't know what you'd do without a mama if she ended up in jail."

"Yeah," I say softly, not bothering to remind Carl that I did end up without Mama. And it was awful. And I never stopped missing her. But also...something new occurs to me. I did okay without her. Better than okay, really.

Mama always said, "Brandee Jean, you just do what I say and everything will be okay."

Most of the time, though, it wasn't.

"BJ?" Alaric gives my arm a squeeze. "You okay?"

I give myself a little shake. Now is not the time to get all misty-eyed about Mama. "Yeah, I'm fine," I tell Alaric. Then I turn to Carl. "Hey, do you remember Shauna?" I ask.

"Your friend? The pretty one?" He tilts his head. "She had a wicked sweet tooth?"

Technically, all my friends were pretty, Mama wouldn't have it any other way. "Ugly rubs off," she'd tell me. "It's a virus."

Even though Mama was dead by the time I met Shauna, I was still living in her house and by her rules.

"Yes, Shauna loves candy," I say, coming back to the conversation. "She ended up..." My throat closes and I can't quite get the words out.

"With the biker gang, the Devil Wings," Carl finishes for me, and I don't bother correcting him—that she was *taken* by them. She wasn't *with* them.

"Once the Pink Pussies took the hint that this was the Devil Wings' territory, they moved on to the next patch of ground. Think they're fighting over the bowling alley now?"

"The bowling alley *was* always the place to be," I say. Alaric snorts but I ignore him.

"But then this new group moved in...the Dead Men. Their vests have skulls on them."

"I haven't heard of them, I say.

"They're new. Vampires. Now *they're* fighting the Devil Wings."

I shake my head. What are the chances that Shauna is even still alive?

"There's been a few of them hanging around the parking lot in the evenings," Carl says. "They're trying to start shit with the Devil Wings."

"Okay, thanks, Carl," I say, when I hear the first rumble of a motorcycle engine.

"There's one now. Should I introduce you?" he asks.

"Is this wise?" Alaric asks, turning to Zahara. She shrugs.

"We're freaking gods. Remember?" I tell him with a wink. "Together, we're like, the strongest thing on the planet.

Carl grabs his shotgun and walks us out, marveling at the door working. "It's a vamp," he shouts over his shoulder. "One of those Dead Men."

The rider spots us and roars to a stop, his tires leaving a black line behind him, and the smell of hot rubber in the air.

"Carl," he says. "It's not safe out here on your own. The store is neutral territory, but not the lot." His eyes are glued to my chest. "Unless you're looking for some danger? I'd be happy to…"

I shoot a lightning bolt into the ground at his feet. I mean, I try to hit just by his feet but it goes a bit astray and hits a nearby stop sign. Same effect and I pretend like I totally did it on purpose.

"I guess you can take care of yourselves," he says.

"My friends want to ask you a few questions," Carl says.

"Ain't you just the prettiest thing…" the biker says, looking at Alaric.

"Bugger off," Alaric tells him. Then turns to Carl. "And you too. I am sick of being eyed up and down like I'm nothing but some tasty little biscuit."

Carl and the biker mumble apologies. It's undercut a bit by the biker adding, "You're even hotter when you're angry."

I'm embarrassed by my own behavior as well. "Alaric, I'm so sorry!"

He takes my hand. "No, BJ, it's okay. I've admired your physical assets often enough."

I can't help but grin at that. "And did you like what you saw?"

"Oh my gods!" Zahara explodes. "Don't make me regret not murdering you both and keeping all the power for myself." Turning to Alaric she puts a finger into his chest. "Can't you tone down the hotness?" she asks. "It's distracting to everyone."

"Is that even possible?" I ask.

"I don't know…but you're not always shooting lightning," Zahara says. "You have to make it happen."

"Let me try." Alaric makes a constipated face, but his concentrating seems to work. I can look at him without wanting to lick his skin.

Zahara grins. "Better. And I'd still hit that."

"Nice trick," the biker says. "What are you?"

"None of your business, vamp." Alaric says, and I'm surprised at the tone of his voice. Athena had told us that the fae and the vampires were at war with one another, but Alaric had never seemed all that into his fae side

The biker hisses, baring his fangs. "You're the ones that wanted to talk with me."

"Be nice," I tell Alaric with a glare. I turn to the biker. "We need information," I tell him. "I'm looking for my friend Shauna. She's with the Devil Wings; they took her."

"Bitch, we're at war with them," he says, sitting up.

"Call her a bitch again and I will make you eat your vest." Alaric says, and I believe him. The vamp does too because he snaps his mouth shut, fangs clicking against his lower teeth.

"This was before the war," I explain. "It would have been right about six months ago. Vampires were just starting to make themselves known."

"Oh, sure. There was a big party around then. We vamps were thinking of joining their gang, but the party went south, fast." He gets to his feet and fishes out a cigarette.

"Would anyone they...captured have been with them?" I ask as he lights the cigarette.

"I guess," he says, pulling on his cigarette. "A lot of people were joining up with them then. They were on full out recruitment. All the new members were there, they had all their old ladies with them"

"Their...grandmas?" I ask.

"No...their women," Carl says. I look at him; I'd almost forgotten he was there. He shrugs. "I watch a lot of Sons of Anarchy."

"Yeah, their girlfriends, wives...I mean, Petey did bring his granny but she was an old lady before she was actually old..."

"What happened?" Alaric asks in his no nonsense voice.

"Everybody was getting along pretty well, if you know what I mean. They didn't even seem to mind we were vamps. But it did get a little rowdy when this lady with big tits— sorry, 'scuse my language—big knockers showed up and started blowing the wings off everyone."

"Uh-huh," Zahara says, and I look to her for an explanation. But she looks like she has no idea what that means, either. I'm afraid it might be a weird sex thing, until the vamp continues.

"Yeah, she was saying she doesn't want to see another fairy as long as she lived, and that got a whole bunch of the guys riled up, saying they ain't no fairies, but then she said… well…" He actually looks horrified. "She said not that kind of fairy, and snapped her fingers and all of a sudden wings just kind of popped out of the backs of all their women, and everybody got to yelling about it, and the woman with the big knockers—sorry—big boobies, started running around, ripping the wings right out of their backs."

"So…the Devil Wings are fae?" I ask. "That's gotta be better, right? The gang that grabbed Shauna aren't vamps, so they're not going to drain her blood, at least."

Alaric shakes his head. "Don't underestimate the fae. They can do just as much or more harm than any vampire." Holding out his hand, Alaric calls up a ball of fire, reminding me of what he can do with his little bit of fae blood.

"He's right," Zahara says. "With the wing description, it sounds like they must be pixies and that's not great either. They can use a person's vitality. You know, vamps drink blood but pixies can take their beauty. Use them up and leave them."

Poor Shauna!

"What happened next?" I demand.

"All these pretty wings were just laying on the ground with bloody stubs sticking out of them," he says, unhelpfully.

"Did the lady with the big…um…did she say who she was?"

"I don't know. When I wasn't looking at her tits…sorry, I mean fun bags, I was looking at those wings…no wait! She said her name was Afro something."

"It was Aphrodite, I'm sure of it," Alaric says. "She'll show up anywhere there's free love, but if she's not the one getting attention, she can get pretty cranky. You saw how she was when it was her test in the competition."

"And a big set of wings is kind of attractive," the guy adds. "I mean, I know we're at war with the pixies, but they are a buncha lookers. This one girl, man…woo…eee." He smiles. "She put up quite the fight. Told Miss Tits R' Us that she wanted a piece of her."

"I'll roll you down a hill," the vamp says, suddenly pitching his voice in a high falsetto, cocking one hip out and placing his hand on it like he's all that.

"What?" I ask. "Say that again."

"I'll roll you down a hill," he repeats, the falsetto still in place, one finger waving in the air. It's a dead-on impression of Shauna, and rolling people down a hill was always her go-to threat.

"Who said that?" I ask. "What did she look like?"

"Pissed," he says. "She wasn't taking no shit from anybody."

Yep, that also sounds like Shauna. I'm about to ask about her hair color, because you can't miss it. She liked to dye her hair a bright cotton candy pink. "Stripper pink," the man says, confirming my suspicions. "Helluva pair on her, too."

"Yeah, her legs are top notch," I say. Shauna is short and cute, but perfectly proportioned.

"Huh? No, her wings!" the guy says. "She had the biggest set of the bunch!

17

I gape. "Shauna. Had wings?" I ask.

"Big beautiful blue ones," the vamp confirms. He takes another puff on his cigarette. "She must be powerful too because Afro-titty ran away after that. Then...well, when there's blood everywhere we vamps get out of hand. We started drinking the fae and that was that. Now we're at war."

Alaric comes up behind me, I can feel his anger at the vamp's mention of drinking fae, but his focus is on me. "Are you okay?" he asks.

"Shauna doesn't need to be saved?" I ask dumbly.

"It sounds like she's pretty comfortable," Carl offers. "Rolling people down hills and popping her wings out for everybody to see."

"But..." I'm so confused. "If she was part of the pixie gang, why..."

Suddenly there's a comforting talon on my shoulder. "BJ," Zahara says, "if your friend Shauna was a pixie, she might have been scoping you out."

"Scoping me out?" I ask. "What do you mean?"

Alaric nods. "Reconnaissance. Pixies feed on beauty, remember? How long have you and Shauna been friends?"

I sniffle, feeling betrayed. "Not long," I admit. "Mama died and I was out scavenging…" I close my eyes trying to remember. "I was hitting up the beauty aisle at some closed-up drugstores. We'd had a bunch of hot days and I wanted to stock up on sunblock. Then while I was there, I was trying on lipstick, picked up a few new eyeliners. Just the basics, of course. I couldn't go crazy."

"Sounds like more than basics," the biker observes.

I glare at him and thunder rumbles.

"But what do I know about that girly stuff?" he quickly amends.

I sigh and continue my story. "That's when Shauna showed up. She needed help finding the perfect red matte lip. It's part of this whole retro/punk vibe she has. We had so much fun, it almost felt like the world was normal again."

It was such a perfect moment. Too perfect, I now realize. And I never even suspected.

The realization of how thoroughly I was fooled comes with a blasting noise in my head, like the earthquakes that started the collapse of civilization are happening all over again.

"What the holy hell?" Alaric asks and I follow his gaze. The world shaking isn't just in my head. The Piggly Wiggly is collapsing.

"My store!" Carl yells as the whole thing vanishes. The pavement of the parking lot cracks and Alaric grabs me and Carl as Zahara shoots into the sky. He teleports us across the street just as the concrete under our feet vanishes. The vampire scrambles back, barely managing to make it to safety.

Where we were moments before is a crater spewing fire

and lava. The moans of tortured souls fill the air, their voices rising up out of it in unison.

"What is that?" I ask, clutching Alaric.

"I don't know," he says. "But it's not good."

"My bike!" the vamp cries out.

"A sinkhole just swallowed half a block and you're worried about your bike?" Carl shouts. "I have nothing left! I worked hard to keep my store neutral territory and now it's gone!"

"You're alive," I tell Carl.

There's another sound, the roar of engines and the screech of wheels.

"Not for long!" the vamp calls out gleefully. "That's my crew rolling in, and don't think I didn't smell the fae on your pretty boyfriend!" His nose scrunches up like there's something foul in the air. "We'll tear him to pieces!"

"Alaric?" I say, leaning against him. It's like Shauna all over again, except this time they're circling me and I…oh wait, I'm a god.

I try to hit them with lightning, but they're moving fast and I'm not very accurate. I thunder in frustration. Carl doesn't want any part of the paranormal battles, and runs off, his voice barely carrying back to me. "Sorry, Brandee Jean! I didn't sign up for this!"

"I didn't either!" I yell at his retreating back, but I don't think he hears me.

Zahara swoops down and plucks a vamp biker from the group, dropping him from up high. He breaks open like a blood bag, and I gag, turning into Alaric's shoulder.

"Zahara can't take them all," he says into my ear. "I should just teleport us out of here."

"And let a gang of vampire bikers run my hometown? No way!" I shout back, just as I see a biker split off from the group, going after Carl.

"Get Carl to safety," I tell Alaric.

"I'm not leaving you!"

"Duh. Come back after. I'm not facing this by myself!"

He actually smiles before his disappears, the dazzling quality of it leaving me a little breathless.

"Did the boys leave you alone, little girl?" someone shouts. One of the bikers decides they've had enough fun trying to scare me and throws a chain. They mean to catch me and drink me dry. The chain wraps around my arm and I grin, shooting a volt of electricity through the metal. It fries the vamp and he falls off his bike.

What is taking Alaric so long? Shouldn't he be able to teleport Carl to safety in a split second? And where is Zahara? She took off flying with a vamp; is she also having trouble? I can heal myself if things get too bad, but if enough vamps have their teeth in me, I don't think I can close up the wounds in time. With the healing power split between all three of us, Athena said it wouldn't have the potency it did when it was just in Zeus.

Vamps are not easy to keep down. The one I fried gets back to his feet and throws a knife at me. It hits me in the shoulder and hurts like a bitch, even though I know it won't kill me. I pull it out and brandish it toward him.

Someone lands at my back and I pray it's Alaric. But a female's voice fills my ears. "You realize you have a big ass sword at your belt, right?"

"Edie!" I cry out. "How are you here?" I throw down the knife and grab my sword. I don't know how to use it, but the vamps don't know that.

"Not important right now. I brought company, though."

The vamps are disappearing off their bikes one by one and I see three new people...no, three new *vampires* have arrived. One is Sophia's mentor, Tina, but I don't recognize the other two. They are quickly dispatching the vamps, mostly by decapitation.

Alaric appears before me. "Get that sword ready," he shouts and teleports away.

"To do what?" I ask, but then he reappears holding a vamp and I swing like it was my trusted sparkly baseball bat and lop off the vamp's head.

The tide has turned and the vampires know it. Edie shifts into a dragon and blows fire at three of them, their bikes exploding underneath them and sending body parts raining down on all of us. The vamp bikers that are left decide it's not worth it, and roar off into the horizon, one of them turning to flip me the bird before he disappears.

"Edie!" I hug her, after she transforms back into a girl. "You saved our butts! How did you know I was in trouble?"

"That would be me," Alaric says, and I raise an eyebrow.

"I got Carl to safety but then I realized we may have the powers of a god, but we're still a bit clueless about this world," Alaric explains. "I know next to nothing about vamps. So I teleported back to Amazon Academy to get some help. Edie was the first one I saw and then we went to Underworld Academy for reinforcements."

"You did all that?" I ask. "You must be exhausted."

"Yeah…" Alaric says. "Now I see why healing goes with Zeus' other powers," he pants.

"Tell me about it," Zahara says, dropping beside us, and looking a little peaked herself. "I'm bushed."

The three friendly vamps come over and I offer Tina a nod. "I'm sorry about Sophia."

"She was a stone-cold bitch," Tina says. "I really liked her."

"I'm Marguerite," the other female vampire introduces herself.

"This is Tina's brother, and my boyfriend, Val," Edie

introduces a tall handsome vampire with a T-shirt that says, *It's the end of the world as we know it and I feel fine.*

"Good job," I tell Edie. "He's a hottie."

"Can someone please tell us what happened here?" Alaric asks.

"Whoa, talk about hotties," Tina says.

"No kidding," adds Marguerite. "I mean, I don't even swing that way, but I'd take a shot."

"Neither do I," says Val, "But if I didn't have a girlfriend I totally would. You are a very attractive man."

"Alaric," I yell, trying not to drool. "Can you please tone down your power again?"

"Oh, right. Yes. Sorry," he says and becomes more like his normal hot self, instead of so hot you would kill for him.

"As Alaric was asking, what is going on with…" I motion toward the fiery gaping hole. I'm at a loss for what to call it. "That?"

We walk to the brink of the crevice, and the heat hits me in the face. I'm really going to have to do a hot oil treatment on my hair after this. Worse, I hadn't just imagined the voices coming from the hole; a symphony of pain and anguish rises up.

"I have never seen anything like this," Edie says.

"It might be…" Tina starts, and Val finishes her sentence.

"A gateway to hell."

"We have to get back and tell the other gods about this," Edie says. "I'd say Hades is up to something."

"Zombie!" Marguerite shouts and hisses. I whirl.

"No wait!" I shout but before I can stop her the vamp has my mama by the throat. I toss a warning bolt at her feet, and actually manage to have decent aim this time. Marguerite drops her hand in shock and I rush in between them.

"This is my mama!" I yell at her.

"Oh. Sorry." She looks around. "My mistake. When I see a

zombie, I go to kill mode." She looks at my mama. "Sorry...ma'am."

"Nice friends you have here, Brandee Jean."

"Mama, why are you here?" I ask, trying to maintain eye contact. She had, in fact hit up Tata's Tops, so Hades must have given her some spending money.

"Sorry baby," Mama says, "but I've got to be the bearer of bad news. Hades is unhappy with the result of the competition and has decided that he wants to destroy the world. Bring hell to earth. He said if Zeus can't have it, nobody can."

"Mama!" I cry. "Can't you talk some sense into him?"

She shakes her head. "No way. There are plenty of dead and undead wandering around down in the underworld since all this fighting broke out. I've got to stay in my place in order to keep it, you get me? And I need to get back to it, make sure some other zombie hottie isn't snuggling up to my man."

She wanders towards the gaping hole, and I grab her wrist. "Be careful, we don't know what that is, or what it can do!"

"Don't be silly," Mama says, patting my wrist. "It's a hellmouth, a portal to the underworld. Since I'm undead now, I can use any of the hellmouths to travel."

"Any of..." Edie says.

"There are more of these things?" Val asks, and Mama nods.

"Alaric," Edie says, snapping into motion, "we need to get back to Amazon Academy and warn the others, right away. Grab the zombie and..."

I whirl. "Don't you touch my mama," I warn.

"Despite their heightened strength, zombies are more delicate than they look. If you break her she won't be able to tell us more," Zahara reasons.

"Plus she is BJ's mom," Alaric adds. At least my god-mates have my back. Edie and the vampires don't look well pleased but I don't care.

"What else?" I ask. "Mama, please give us something to go on."

She looks nervous, peeking into the hellmouth as if scared someone will see her talking to us.

"Alright, baby girl," she finally says. "But listen close because I'm only saying this once. The next hellmouth is opening in London, near your boyfriend's family estate. Hades is going to send a wave of zombies to attack if the negotiations don't work."

"What negotiation?" Alaric demands.

"The one between your father and brother," she says.

"Trevor?" I ask. "But he's dead!"

"Hades made him into a zombie," Mama tells me. "Hades says he's too useful to be dead."

"If Hades is bringing hell to earth, why would he care about my family estate?" Alaric asks, clearly shaken by the news that his recently deceased loved one is now the undead. I can relate. We've all been there.

"No one wants to live in a fiery hellscape," my mama explains. "Hades thinks a fancy country home is just the thing...and he's willing to spare your family if you agree to serve him."

Alaric shakes his head, uncertain. "I can't say what my father would do in the face of that proposition."

"Mama, can we stop it? Will you keep feeding us information?" I ask. "Oh baby," Mama says, one hand caressing my cheek. "I didn't come so you can stop it," she tells me. "I came to help you make the right decision. You must give up your powers and bow to Hades. He's willing to let you keep the crown and the title of princess. Isn't that exciting, baby? You'll finally be the little princess I always wanted."

"Mama!" I yell louder than I mean to, but seriously? Does she not see how messed up this is? "Mama," I repeat, softer this time. "I don't need to be a crappy princess anymore. I'm a god."

"No, baby, you're not." She looks at me with pity in her eyes. It's the same way she looked when explaining that I would never shop in the petite section of the store. "Hades is the one true king of the gods."

18

____

"Mama, no," I say. "Hades is not a good guy! He's a bad boyfriend and a worse god!"

She backs away to the edge of the hellmouth. "So should I tell Hades you agree to serve him?" she asks. "You've always let me make the decisions when it came to my boyfriends. Remember when Timothy insisted we observe the lord's day? You were such a trooper coming to church with us every week."

"But it turned out he just wanted to steal from the collection plate, Mama. Remember that?" I shake my head. "This time, I can't just look the other way and pretend I don't see him taking money out instead of putting it in. And I'm not gonna believe him when he says he's just helping them keep count. This is about more than just the fate of the Beaver Lick Christian Chapel and Drive-Thru. This affects the whole world. So no, Mama, we will not bow to Hades."

Alaric comes to my right and Zahara my left. They're in agreement. There's no way we're going to let Hades take over the world.

Mama closes her eyes and shakes her head. When she

opens them, they're filled with sadness; as usual, she's completely bought whatever her man has been selling her

"I'll tell him you're thinking about it. It just sounds nicer." She steps back and disappears into the fire pit.

"Mama!" I yell and rush forward but Alaric pulls me back.

"She's fine, she's returning to Hades," Zahara says.

"So...should I have ripped off her head?" Marguerite asks.

"Not helping," Tina tells her.

"We need to get back to Amazon Academy right now," Edie says.

"Oh no, I'm going to England," Alaric tells us.

"We have to warn the other gods!" Val says. "A hellmouth is not something you can just ignore until it goes away."

"Tell me about it," Marguerite says, peering over the edge. "It looks like an STD. My girlfriend is basically a doctor and she works in a free clinic for supernaturals. She's told me some stories..."

"Again," Tina elbows her. "Not helping."

"I'm going with Alaric," I tell them. "He saw that Wisconsin was in trouble and he came here to help save my hometown. I'm doing the same for him. If Hades thinks he can just take over my super-hot boyfriend's English manor, then I...oh my gods, can we live there, Alaric? Like later, when the world isn't ending?"

"Perhaps," he shrugs. "But first we'll have to kick out the god of the dead, and his consort, who happens to be your mother."

"And I thought my family was messed up," Val says.

"Okay," Zahara steps up. "Edie and the vamps, return to Amazon Academy and report what we've discovered about the seismic activity and Hades."

"And you?" I ask.

"Oh, I'm not leaving you two. The power of Zeus is in all three of us. We have to stick together." She hesitates and then adds, "Also, I'm very close to laying some eggs and I'd rather it be in England than Wisconsin." She turns to me. "No offense, BJ, but...she waves her arms around indicating the post-apocalyptic hellscape.

"Wait a minute," I say. "Is laying some eggs similar to slamming a doot? Because I agree, between the motorcycle gangs and this hellmouth thing, Wisconsin has seen enough shit today."

Alaric clears his throat. "Brandee, I believe that Zahara is telling us that she's going to be a mother."

"What?" I screech. "Holy chickens coming home to roost! And who's the lucky father?"

"No father," Zahara says with a shake of her head. "Harpies are a self-fertilizing species."

"A whuh?"

Zahara sighs. "We don't need no man to make no babies."

"Ooooh!" I say. "Wow. Weird, but cool." Then something else occurs to me. "Oh wait, you got virility plus you can make babies by yourself...and we've been gods for less than a day and you're already..." As all the pieces come together and I fully understand what this means, I can't help but throw my arms around Zahara and squeeze her tight as I can. "Your poor vagina is gonna be so stretched out with all the babies that are gonna shoot out of you."

Alaric peels me away from Zahara. "We can all heal, remember? I'm sure Zahara's..." He clears his throat loudly.

"Hoo hoo," Val offers, and Edie smacks him on the arm.

"Her lady bits will be just fine," finishes Alaric.

"It seems like you have all decided to head off to the UK, then," Edie says. "But remember that we're just paranormals. You guys are the actual gods. We can report to the council at Amazon Academy, but no decisions can be made until you are there."

"Then let's get things moving." Alaric steps forward and

tells Edie and the vamps to all hold hands. In a flash they're gone and he's back.

"Ready?" he asks, grabbing my hand in his, I hold Zahara's talon with my other one.

"Are you?" I ask.

"No," he says. "I wasn't ready for any of this, but here goes."

In an instant we are no longer in a crumbling Wisconsin hellscape but a well manicured country estate, surrounded by rolling green hills. Before us is a house. No, not a house, a mansion.

I turn around and gardens sprawl behind us, everything perfectly in place and blooming beautifully. It would be perfect if it weren't for the huge gaping hellmouth right in the center of it. I whistle.

"This is your home?" I ask. I'm suddenly super glad I just showed him the Piggly Wiggly, and not the falling down place where I lived.

Alaric reddens. Zahara tilts her head. "Judging from the architecture it looks like that manor house was built sometime in the Victorian era."

"It is like Downton Abbey up in here," I say.

"Let's just...go inside," he says. He leads us across the lawn and to the main door. He knocks, but no one answers. "Strange. The doorman never leaves his post."

"How many servants do you have?" I ask.

"Not many...only twenty or so. For a house this big that's a skeleton crew. We have more in the summer."

I look at Zahara. "Do you believe this?"

"No. I can't." She shakes her head. "They should really hire more. My family's palace is about this size and we have fifty servants."

I gape. For some reason I forgot that Zahara was also royalty. A Marquessa. I straighten my shoulders and remind myself that even though I might not come from a great bloodline like they do, I still clawed my way to the top to share the ultimate power with them.

Alaric gives up on knocking and opens the door on his own. It swings on its hinges, making an ominous screech that echoes through the empty foyer. Everything is perfect here, just like it was in the garden, but it's also very…empty. Family portraits of people long dead stare down from the walls, but they're the only people to be seen.

"Okay, now I am getting a gothic horror vibe," I say. "If a woman in black appears, I'm going to light this place up."

"We just need to find my family," Alaric says, not quite able to keep the worry out of his voice. I want to remind him that we're gods, and that together, we can take on anything. Then I remember the look on Mama's face as she descended into the hellmouth, and I get it.

I'm a god, too. That doesn't mean I don't worry about my family.

"Hello?" Alaric calls, his voice reverberating. "Mother? Father? Is anybody here?"

Zahara's talon finds my hand, and I squeeze her back, glad to know I'm not the only one freaked out by this empty, really nicely decorated place.

"Let's try the study," Alaric says, and leads us down a hall to a set of double doors, which creak just like the front door did when he opens them.

A man sits at a desk. I see some of Alaric in him. He has my boyfriend's broad shoulders, and his jawline, but there's a glint of meanness in his eyes. A slim woman sits on a nearby couch, sipping wine. She must be Trevor's mother, Alaric's stepmother. Trevor's there too, in the flesh. Well, in his rotting undead flesh.

"Brother," Trevor says with a sigh. "I did not expect you so soon. Hades seemed to think the piece he keeps on the side could keep you busy in Wisconsin a little longer. Long enough for me to convince them to bend the knee to Hades, anyway."

"What are you doing?" Alaric asks. He whirls on his father. "You can't sell out our family to Hades. The manor has been in our name for generations. Don't let him come in here with his horde of undead and bespoil our home!"

"Hey, my mama is one of those undead," I remind Alaric, and his father's eyes shift to me, running up and down my body with a sneer.

"I'm not giving anyone my home," Alaric's father shouts. "Who is this riffraff, Alaric?" He looks at Zahara with disgust on his face. "And what is this thing?"

"This *thing* is going to claw out your eyes—" Zahara starts but Alaric steps forward.

"I won the competition, Father," he says.

His father brightens. "You did? Then send this Hades fellow packing. We already offered up our servants to him, as a sacrifice."

"You did what?" I ask, horrified.

"Oh dear, an American." Trevor's mother wrinkles her nose.

"Mother, this is Brandee Jean. She's quite a laugh once you get used to her crassness," Trevor says. "She's also got a heck of a rack on her."

I glare at him. "At least I'm not sending innocent people to the slaughter. How could you sacrifice your employees?"

"It bought us some time in the negotiation," Trevor says. His bright eyes look from Alaric to me to Zahara. "Brother, why don't you tell our father the truth. You did not actually win the competition."

"Did you or didn't you?" Alaric's father demands.

"I did...but Brandee and Zahara also won."

His father glowers. "You tied with an American and

a...whatever this creature is? I have never been more disappointed in you."

"Oh! The eggs are coming!" Zahara suddenly cries out, arms wrapped around her midsection. She turns to Alaric. "Where's a good place to keep my clutch safe and warm and dry?"

"Dear lord, what is happening?" Alaric's stepmom demands, shooting to her feet, wine spilling over her fingers.

Alaric looks to Trevor. "The hellmouth opening won't affect the actual house, right? Because Hades wants it, right? It won't expand and take our home with it?"

Trevor looks from Zahara to Alaric. "Brother, did you knock up the harpy? Are these your little children getting ready to be laid?" he asks, gleefully malicious.

Their father's face reddens at the thought and he looks like he's about to go off on another tirade but instead downs a glass full of brown liquor.

Trevor suddenly blinks and scrubs at his eyes. "Furthermore, when did you get so good looking? I honestly thought you peaked in ninth grade when you finally got your braces off." Trevor sends a wink my way. "You may want to consider sending his orthodontist a thank you note. Alaric had a hell of an overbite. If it hadn't been fixed, I don't know that you'd be getting the same tongue to tongue action with him."

"Trevor!" Alaric's dad snaps. "Enough of your foolishness. This is not the time!"

"No, Father," Trevor smiles. "It never is, is it?"

Alaric and Zahara are gone, I realize suddenly. And it seems like Trevor may have actually helped distract his father and mother. Or at least shifted their annoyance to him.

"Alaric was really upset when you popped like a balloon," I tell him now.

He shrugs one shoulder. "Of course, he was. Him and his bloody bleeding heart. But what about you, my fair Brandee Jean? There was once a spark between us. Did you mourn what might have been?"

"Not really, no." I fold my arms. "You were acting like a real turd on the island."

Amazingly, Trevor smiles at this. "I was a total tosser, wasn't I?" He eyes me. "I like your shiny new sword."

"Thanks, we all got one. You could have had one too, if you hadn't been so selfish."

He shakes his head. "I placed my bets poorly. Hades and Zeus seemed like sure winners. Frankly, I grew tired of them fairly quickly, but the promises made were of the binding sort. I always fancied myself the type able to squirm out of any situation, but that one was beyond me."

I can't believe it, but I almost feel sorry for Trevor. "Was croaking sort of a relief then?"

Trevor laughs. "No, dying wasn't a relief. Finding out that Hades upgraded me to a zombie, however, was a nice surprise. And once he becomes the god of everything he'll command a witch to make some sort of anti-decomposition potion for me and the rest of his loyal zombie crew." He slants a knowing look my way. "Including your momzbie, I assume."

"So you're back to kissing Hades' ass," I observe.

"It seems that way," Trevor agrees at the same time that Alaric and Zahara reappear, a girl I don't recognize alongside them. She has shiny blonde hair, and big blue eyes that go even wider when they land on me.

"Oh! You are so pretty!" She crosses the distance between us and immediately begins petting me. Suddenly, I understand dogs. I want to push my head into her hand and have her groom me all day. But first, I should probably get her name.

"I'm Brandee Jean," I say.

"Brandee Jean, the new high queen," the girl says cheerily.

"And you are…?" I prompt.

"I'm Cassie, and I've got to say, thanks for killing Mr. Zee…again. Edie thought she'd done the job herself, but I guess gods are hard to kill, right? I mean, that's a good thing now, because you're a god, and I like you."

"Wait…" I'm confused. Since Zahara got the "all knowing" part of the god gig, I guess the occasional bout of cluelessness will still be one of my personality quirks. Being a god doesn't take care of all your deficiencies. "You know Edie?"

"Yes," Cassie says. "I know Edie from Mount Olympus Academy. It's closed down now, what with the world ending, and everything—we sure are sorry about that. But Mr. Zee… he had to go. We didn't know it would cause well…stuff like that."

She points out the window facing the hellmouth, where steam is continuously rising.

"Excuse me," Trevor's mom rises from the couch, apparently finding the arrival of another stranger to be too much. "I'm going to have to ask all of you to leave my home."

"My home, Bellaria," Alaric's dad says, gruffly. "This is *my* ancestral home, not yours."

"Yes, Padric, but it is my inheritance that has quite literally kept the roof over our heads. I didn't spend several thousand pounds on improvements just to have these sort of"—her nose scrunches together with disgust as she motions toward us— "*people* in it."

"I'm not a person," Zahara says, her chin sticking out. "I'm a harpy, and a very pregnant one. I'm just going to go lay my eggs in the ballroom, if that's okay."

"It certainly is not!" Padric says, his face going beet red.

"I'm so sorry," Cassie says, coming to his side and taking

his hand. Reluctantly, he lets her. This girl has a way about her. I was melting under her hands the second she touched my hair. I'd say there's a paranormal element to her gift, but my god senses tell me there isn't. She's just so sweet and genuine, you can't help but like her.

"We didn't mean to crash your place," Cassie goes on. "But a harpy nest has a very powerful magic. Zahara has already excreted her pheromones here, so the babies must be raised where they can smell their mother while they are growing up."

"She did what?" Bellaria demands, sending Zahara a piercing glance. "I will not have this atrocity under my roof, raising a brood!"

"Oh, you won't!" Cassie goes over to Trevor's mom. "Zahara is much too busy to raise her own children. She's a god, you know. One third of the most powerful god-trio in the universe. Your son, Alaric, showed up with her at Amazon Academy, thinking it would be a safe place for her to spawn."

"To…spawn?" Bellaria repeats.

"Yes," Cassie nods brightly. "But unfortunately Zahara has already marked this place as her nest."

"Yeah, sorry about that," Zahara says. "Total pheromone thing, out of my control. Happened as soon as we got here."

"And so," Cassie continues, "my friend Edie suggested that your son collect me, and bring me back here to your lovely home. I will tend to the eggs, and see to their proper raising and training while their mother is busy ruling the world with your son and Brandee Jean."

Suddenly interested, Padric comes to Cassie's side. "And these…offspring. Will they inherit anything from their mother?"

"Just good looks," Zahara says, to which Trevor stifles a giggle.

"Father," Alaric says. "If you're asking if there will be benefits to you raising the children of a goddess on your property, you can assume the answer is yes."

Zahara nods. "Edie assures me that Cassie will be the perfect den mother, but I would not dream of leaving my first-hatched brood here without protection. You will have 24/7 protection from a cohort of harpies in the sky above, and I will also be dispatching at least a dozen Amazons to enforce safety on the ground."

Padric claps his hands together, turning to Bellaria. "You see? We don't have to give up anything to this Hades character. With harpies and Amazons on our side, we can hold onto our home."

Irritated, Trevor crosses his arms. "You're forgetting that Hades is a god as well, Father. He wants the powers these three have."

"Speaking of things being inside of someone," Zahara says, her face contorting as she clutches her midsection again.

"It's time!" Cassie says, snapping to attention. "I'll need warm towels, at least three pillows, and probably a mop."

"A mop?" Trevor's mom asks, and I realize she probably doesn't know what one is, and certainly can't locate it now that they handed all their servants over to Hades.

"Yes," Cassie says. "Also—"

But she doesn't get to finish. Suddenly, her eyes roll back into her head, showing only whites.

"Oh my gods!" I shout, running over to her. "I think she's having a seizure!"

"No, wait," Alaric intercepts me, grabbing my hand. "Edie said Cassie is a seer. You won't be able to interrupt her if she's in a trance."

Cassie's mouth gapes open and a voice that is not her own emerges from her throat.

"Divided they fall, united they rule. The three must stand against the one. Each of the three will sacrifice to the one. It must be so."

Cassie's eyes come back to the forefront, bright blue and aware. "That was a pretty good one, right?"

"It was dramatic," Zahara agrees.

Bellaria has clearly had enough. "I'm going to up to my suites. I will be taking a Xanax and do not want to be disturbed until the hellmouth in the east garden is gone." With that she sweeps out of the room, head held high.

"Great seeing you, Mom," Trevor says ironically. My eyes meet his. I realize that while my mama might be a Momzbie and his is a cold aristocratic bitch, they have quite a bit in common. Which gives Trevor and me something in common too.

"Cassie," Alaric says. "The three must stand against the one... Does that mean us against Hades?"

Cassie shrugs. "I don't know. I'm only the messenger."

"Don't forget the best part," Trevor says. *"Each of the three will sacrifice to the one."*

"It must be so," Alaric repeats, brooding.

"Doesn't sound like you guys come out on top, after all," Trevor says, moving to the door. "If you all are going to sacrifice to Hades in the end, my work here is done. Dad, I'll be wanting my old room back. And hire some more servants, in the meantime. Hades will have this place operating at high capacity, if he chooses it for his headquarters. We'll need everything shipshape!"

He stops with his hand on the doorknob, his eyes meeting mine. "I really am sorry that you chose the wrong side, BJ." There's a sadness in his smile for a second that reminds me of the Trevor I knew at Amazon Academy, a guy who was definitely an asshole, but like I said about Wisconsin…he was *my* asshole.

"I think we could've been a good team, too," Trevor says. "But it's not over yet." He flashes his teeth at Alaric. "May the best man win!"

With that he leaves, his footsteps making soft squishing noises as he goes out the back door, his zombie feet just about having put in all the steps they can manage. He'll need a new body soon, something I'm sure Hades will be happy to supply him with, just like he did my mama. I almost feel sad, thinking about it. Will I even know Trevor the next time I see him?

We all watch through the window as Trevor approaches the hellmouth and executes a perfect swan dive. It closes behind him with a rumble.

"Hey guys," Zahara says. "I know a portal to hell just closed and all that, but could I get a hand over here?"

"Yes! Of course, my dear," Padric is suddenly very helpful and protective of Zahara, now that he knows she's got an army of harpies and Amazons to back his play. He escorts her out of the room, Cassie and Bellaria following.

"Well," I sigh, looking to Alaric. "United we stand, right?"

"Yes," Alaric says, taking my hand. "United we stand."

And even though he's smiling, I feel the worry underneath it, because I've got the same niggling fear in the back of my mind, too.

Each of the three will sacrifice to the one.

19

"**N**ice of you to drop by," Athena says acidly, the moment we teleport to Amazon Academy.

"That's my fault," Zahara says, slipping into her seat next to my throne. "I was, you know, giving birth. It's a whole thing."

"I wouldn't know," Athena says, waiting as I take my throne and Alaric slides into his folding chair on my right side. I'm still not okay with this setup.

"What happened while we were gone?" I ask Athena.

"A lot," she says, frowning. "I've summoned the war council; they're in the next room."

"Summoned them meaning that you also appointed them, I assume," Alaric says. "Since we weren't consulted."

"There wasn't time," Athena says briskly, her eyes bouncing off his to mine. "If one of you had stayed behind to approve—"

"We had to go," I say quickly, cutting her off.

"And it's a good thing we did," Zahara adds.

"A seer gave us a prophecy," Alaric explains. *"Divided they fall, united they rule. The three must stand against the one. Each of the three will sacrifice to the one. It must be so."*

Athena frowns. "That's disturbing, to say the least. If you all must stay together, you will need to give some of the council the power to make decisions in your name. I would advise that each of you have a stand-in that you trust."

"I would like Priyanka, my roommate from the contest. She had a good head on her shoulders even if she couldn't control her thunder," Zahara says fairly quickly.

"You knew her for like two days," I remind Zahara.

She shrugs. "I have good instincts about people. For example, I knew from the moment I met you, that you were gonna be trouble."

"Ha, ha," I grumble and then turn to Alaric. "What about you?"

To my surprise he blushes a little. "Er, I have someone in mind, but I'm not sure how you'll feel about it."

"Is it one of your family members," I ask, wondering if I'm going to have to tell him full out how horrible they all are. It feels a little early in our relationship for that.

"No," Alaric says. "It's actually my ex-girlfriend. Charlotte Bexley Wessex of the London branch, not the rowdier York ones, of course. Unlike her cousins, Bex would never email a thank you note. Or speak to someone across the table at a dinner party. Such crassness horrifies her."

"Wait, those things are crass?" I ask.

"Well, yes, for people of my..." Realizing he's treading into dangerous waters, Alaric clears his throat and switches back to talking about Bex. "But she's not only the personification of class, she's discreet, great in an emergency, and—"

"Okay," I interrupt. "Please stop talking now. I've got the picture. She's perfect. Why'd you even break up with her?"

Alaric goes even redder and I realize...

"She broke up with you?" I narrow my eyes at him. "Are

you just bringing her here so she can see that you're extra super hot now and have an amazing new girlfriend? Is this an eat your heart out move?"

"No!" Alaric looks legitimately shocked. "It's just when Athena mentioned the war council, hers was the first name that came to mind."

"Don't second-guess yourself," Athena unapologetically butts into our conversation. "This Bex girl sounds qualified and clearly you trust her. I'll have her summoned." Athena looks to me. "And your choice, Brandee Jean?"

I cross my arms over my chest, feeling a little pouty. "Well I got some ex-boyfriends I might wanna call up too. Jimmy 'Jimbo' Barnwall was famous for pissing his name in the snow—in cursive. Of course, that ended when he went out in minus-twenty-degree weather and lost the tip of his penis to frostbite."

Athena raises her eyebrows. "Perhaps his judgment isn't the best."

"Maybe not," I agree. "But then there was also Steve Lowell. He played hockey, mostly 'cause he liked to fight. Actually he's not a great choice; we ended things after he decided a girl named BJ ought to give him a...well, you know. I punched him in the junk so hard he had to walk around with an ice pack for the entire next week."

"Does any man get out of a relationship with his junk intact?" Zahara laughs. "Alaric ,you may want to consider some protective gear for down below."

"Don't listen to her, Alaric! Those were just two boys and I've dated at least a dozen or more. All the rest of their man bits are fine." I frown, recalling... "Well, actually, Jackson Daniels and I were playing with his BB gun in eighth grade...But you know, he's fine. Boys only need one working testicle."

"Reassuring," Alaric says softly.

"Enough!" Athena breaks in. "Brandee Jean. Your choice now please, without further commentary."

"Edie," I say immediately.

Athena nods. "Very well. I had assumed you would ask for Edie in your stead," she tells me. "And have already appointed her to the war council. Are you ready to begin?"

"Yeah," I say, sliding down from my throne. "Except for one more thing. This whole setup has got to go."

"This whole setup?" Athena asks, eyebrows coming together in confusion.

"This thing about me having a throne and Alaric and Zahara getting folding chairs. United we stand, remember? I know you favor me because I'm an Amazon, but that crap stops here. It's like Mama always said, Ohio judges going to vote for Ohio girls, and Indiana judges are going to vote for Indiana girls, and Illinois judges—"

"I think I get it," Athena says, stopping me with a hand. "No favorites."

"No favorites," I agree, and instantly their chairs change into thrones as big as mine, but each designed to match their personalities, and their swords. Zahara's is jet black with sharp edges and I'm afraid she'll cut herself, but she roosts in just fine. Alaric's is silver, with straight lines and beautiful, classy scrollwork.

"Very well," Athena sighs, clearly irritated at the change. "Anything else?"

I narrow my eyes at her. "What does the war council room look like?"

Athena rolls her eyes. "It's a rectangle, okay? It's a rectangle and I have you sitting at the head of it."

"Change it," I say. "I want a round table. And…and I want to sit next to Alaric." Okay, so that last bit was dumb, but my man is super hot and for all I know there are some sexy little nymphs in there that might try to crawl under the table and get at what's mine. Not to mention this Bex character.

Also, I just want to sit next to him. I blush a little, thinking about how silly I am to make demands to sit next to my boyfriend when I'm one of the most powerful beings in the universe. But…I want what I want.

Athena excuses herself and leaves the room. Zahara slips her talon into my hand. Her eyes well up with tears and she quickly wipes them away. "Sorry, it's the pregnancy hormones. My emotions are all over the place." She gives me a tremulous smile. "But still, that was touching. You didn't have to do that."

"No," I say. "I'm guessing none of us will ever have to do anything we don't want to do, ever again," I tell her. "But I wanted to. I've seen way too many friendships go the wrong way when there was crown on the line. Divided we fall."

Zahara nods and Alaric leans into me. "I want to sit next to you, too," he whispers. I'm giggling when Athena comes in and announces that the council is ready for us.

As promised, the table is a circle. Athena had appointed her own choices in our absence—herself, Lilliana the Amazon who hated me at first, but then was totally on my side. Also, the goddess Artemis, and a woman I don't recognize who is introduced as Fern. But Edie is there, and so is a girl I'm assuming is Bex, and Priyanka, Zahara's old roommate.

The three of us take our seats—just regular chairs, not thrones—and Athena clears her throat to begin the meeting.

"Let me catch you up to speed," she says. "The vampires and the fae are at full blown war. The Midwest is practically on lockdown. Humans are cowering in their homes, too frightened to leave in case they get caught in the crossfire."

"Yes," Zahara says. "We saw some action in Wisconsin. The motorcycle gangs were out of control."

"They need to be contained," Athena says stiffly. "Humans may only be humans—"

"Hey!" I object, but she plows over me.

"But they still outnumber us." Athena goes on. "The barrier between the paranormal world and their world was only recently broken. Humans are still reeling, but once they're over the shock, they're going to want their world back. And there are a lot more of them than there are of us."

"Why is that?" I ask. "I mean, I just watched Zahara drop about twelve kids in two seconds."

"In order to remain hidden," Athena answers, "paranormals have found it prudent in the past to purposely keep their numbers low. Humans might catch a glimpse of a werewolf, or a vampire, but not often, partly because there were so few of us."

"The greatest trick the Devil ever pulled was convincing the world he didn't exist," Bex says in a quiet yet obviously cultured voice. Everyone looks her way. "Forgive me," she adds. "I spoke out of turn."

"As long as you don't speak nonsense, your voice is welcome here," Athena says.

"She didn't speak nonsense," Alaric says, quickly jumping to Bex's defense. Of course, that's just the type of chivalrous guy he is, right? It doesn't mean that he still has feelings for her. I hope.

"Calm yourself, Alaric," Athena reprimands. "I didn't say she spoke nonsense. In fact, I agree with your Bex."

"Not his Bex," I jump in quickly. "His advisor."

Athena glares at me. "Brandee Jean, English may not be my native language, but I've been speaking it for many thousands of years more than you. Do not presume to correct me again."

Bex stands. "Forgive me. I was afraid that my history with Alaric would make my presence here difficult. It was not my intention to create this unfortunate conversational digression."

I stand as well, 'cause I don't like this Bex person looking down on me.

She looks exactly like I expected her to. Tall, skinny, and flat chested. Her hair is shiny and held back from her face with a delicate velvet headband. She's beautiful in a way that's understated instead of flashy. But beyond her good looks, she has the poise of a pageant girl who's already won every crown there is and feels no need to prove herself. I've actually never met a pageant girl like that. Usually we're all white teeth, tight bottoms, and lifted tits—with an endless well of gaping need beneath that.

Even though I won the biggest crown of all, there will always be a part of me that will feel the need to prove myself to people like Bex. Which is exactly what I do now.

"Bex...I can call you Bex, right? I'm Brandee Jean, BJ for short. If you hadn't noticed, I'm one of the gods here. Along with Alaric." I give his arm a possessive squeeze.

"And me," Zahara adds wryly.

"Right, and Zahara," I say, and then pull Alaric closer. "But really, he and I work together closely. And sometimes we do more than work. If you know what I mean."

"She knows what you mean," Alaric says in a low voice to me.

"Everyone knows what you mean," Edie laughs.

"Brandee Jean, if I might be so bold as speak forthrightly," Bex says in her soft yet clear voice.

Oh this girl! That calm tone isn't fooling me. "Are you saying I spoke forth*wrongly*?"

Beside me Alaric groans.

"Brandee Jean, you are embarrassing yourself," Athena snaps. "But more importantly, you are embarrassing the Amazons."

"I respectfully disagree," Lilliana raises a hand. "An Amazon claims what's hers and that's what our Queen is doing."

"I do not want Alaric!" Bex raises her voice almost like she's a normal girl. Her eyes bug out in a way that's reassuringly unattractive. "He's lovely, of course," she adds, modulating her volume levels. "But I always found him to be a bit boring." She sends an apologetic look Alaric's way. "Sorry."

I realize that I sorta just forced Alaric to publicly relive his breakup with Bex. Giving him arm a pat, I look up at him to see how he's taking it. He's got on his stoic face, which either means he's fine or totally devastated. It's difficult to say.

"Am I boring?" he finally asks, sounding truly perplexed, like the idea has never occurred to him.

"Not even a little bit," I assure him and he gives me that heart melting smile.

"Moving on!" Athena declares, sounding more than a little annoyed. "As we were discussing, when only fringe humans believed in paranormals, they could live in relative peace. Now, with everyone tossed into existence together—"

"All bets are off," Zahara says. "If there's one thing humans are good at, it's mass extinction. Once humans are over the shock of knowing we're real, they're going to come after us. Which means I'll be dropping another dozen kids every chance I get. We need to increase our numbers—and fast."

"No, Zahara." Her advisor, Priyanka, thumps the table.

Priyanka was the first of us contestants to go out, but it was mostly on technicality. She inherited Zeus' thunder and had a hard time controlling it. I was bummed when she exited the contest. I'd been wanting to ask her what it was like being a witch. And about this whole women-in-charge village she comes from. Mama always said there was a thin line between being a strong woman and a ball-buster. I wondered which the women she'd been raised by were.

"Have more children if you want them," Priyanka says to Zahara. "But any attempt to compete with humans by increasing the number of paranormals will be disastrous for women. Every witch, shifter, mermaid, or manticore with a womb will be turned into a broodmare."

Zahara thinks about this for a moment, then nods. "You are right, increasing our population is not the way to go." She frowns. "But I still do not like being outnumbered. My kind more than others will be hated by humans, who will not be able to look past our claws."

"She's right," Edie says. "I thought I was just another girl for a very long time, and I was scared to death when Hermes came to take me to Mount Olympus Academy. I actually attacked him with a letter opener."

She smiles at the memory, but it fades quickly. "Athena knows what she's talking about. With fae at war with vampires—and that's just one element of everything that's gone wrong—the Midwest could become the staging area for a much bigger battle. Humans against Non-Humans, and they won't stop until all of us are dead."

"But, wait," I say. "You said it yourself—you thought you were just a human girl, right?"

"Yes," Edie agrees. "I didn't find out I was dragon until I was at MOA."

"And trust me, Edie," I tell her, flashing a smile. "No human would want to kill you. I mean…well…some girls would kill for those legs, but about thirteen thousand five hundred and twenty six male humans would defend you in a second. I mean, you're hot."

"And you," I turn to Alaric. "You're part fae, but no one

would guess it. And we've already seen that your hotness works on both women and men."

"Wow, I'm screwed," says Zahara, and the whole table laughs.

"Maybe at first glance," I tell her. "But no human who got to know you would ever want to harm you."

I remember how she had lovingly tapped each egg as we left England, her face transformed into beauty with motherly love.

"So, what are you suggesting, Brandee Jean, beauty queen?" Athena asks. "That we let all the hot paranormals serve as ambassadors?"

"Hey, look, being hot doesn't hurt, okay? Beauty opens doors, Mama always said, and if you've got a nice set of tits, someone will hold it for you, too."

The table laughs again, and I smile at them. "I think sending some of the more attractive representatives of each paranormal species to speak to the human leadership is just common sense."

"And the rest?" Athena asks. "What about vampires that attack humans? They can be hot and still be horrible examples of their species."

There's a murmur of agreement.

"Of course," Alaric says. "I'll be the first to admit that my brother Trevor was not ugly—"

"Nope," Zahara agrees, a little too quickly, and Alaric shoots her a glance.

"But he's a despicable person," Alaric finishes.

"Yep," Zahara agrees again. "And Athena is bringing up a good point. There are bad paranormals and good paranormals. We can appoint some of the more attractive, benevolent ones to serve as representatives to humans. It will take time, but eventually revealing the kind natures of the less attractive paranormals—harpies, minotaurs, and the like

—will help humans to live side by side among those of us who wish them no harm."

"And the ones that do wish harm? Like my brother?" Alaric asks.

"Well, why not treat them just like people?" I ask. "I mean, think about it. We already have a system in place for this in the human world. If you hurt another person, you go to jail." I shrug. "Why can't we do the same thing for paranormals?"

Athena shakes her head. "A human prison could never hold a paranormal."

"No," Edie agrees. "It couldn't. But there are paranormal precedents for this. My sister, Mavis, was imprisoned for a while at MOA. Zee put a magical collar on her so that she couldn't shift into her cat form and slip out of her cell."

Sitting forward, Alaric muses. "We could establish a paranormal prison for those of their species that misbehave in the human world?"

"Sure," I say. "Why not?"

Alaric shakes his head. "It's not a bad idea, BJ. But here's the thing—there's no place on Earth that humans are going to agree for us to build this thing. No one is going to want that in their backyard."

"Oh!" Edie cries out. "But what if it's not on Earth?"

"Excuse me?" Athena says, and she sounds so much like Trevor's mom that I have to double check Bellaria didn't follow us here.

"What if it's *under* the Earth?" Edie asks, eyes alight. "Think about it. The three magical academies—Mount Olympus Academy, Amazon Academy and Underworld Academy—all existed as places for paranormals to send their teen children. MOA is closed now, but Underworld Academy is still enrolling students, although I've heard their numbers are way down. Nobody wants to go to school when there's so much fun to be had on earth."

"If you can call them students," Athena sniffs. "And if you call that an Academy. More like a 24/7 frat party."

"I know," Edie agrees. "I've been there. But what I'm saying is: it already exists. There's a cafeteria and plenty of halls that can serve as prison blocks. It's underground, hidden from human eyes and—judging by the fact that nobody has ever shown up down there, despite the really loud parties—deep enough that the noise doesn't rise to the surface."

I find myself nodding in agreement, super excited. "Edie's right! We don't have to build a place to keep the paranormals that hurt humans. And we don't have to hide them, either. It already exists. We just need to turn it from Underworld Academy into Underworld Reformatory."

"And wrest it completely from Hades' hands," Athena says drily. "You forgot that part."

"Oh, no I didn't," I say, taking Alaric's hand in one of mine, and Zahara's talon in the other. "That's what I'm looking forward to the most."

20

The War Council takes a break, promising to reconvene the next day. I realize that I'm exhausted, but when I lay down to take a nap, I can't fall asleep. It could be because I'm hungry…I haven't eaten in, like, two days, which isn't a huge leap for a beauty pageant girl, but usually by now I'd be digesting my own stomach lining, and feeling that pain. Instead, I feel fine, and I'm lying awake in the richly appointed bedroom that Athena gave me, staring at the ceiling when I realize…

"Gods," I say, clapping my hand to my forehead. "I probably don't have to sleep anymore. Or eat!"

It's actually kind of depressing. I love sleeping. My bed back in Wisconsin had something like twenty or thirty throw pillows—all in the shapes of hearts and lips—and I would flop onto them often, zoning out for as many hours as I could in between waxing and tanning appointments.

I'm going to miss sleeping.

And eating…there was always something a little comforting in putting away pizza after a successful crown run, even if I knew Mama would make me pay for it on the stair climber at the YMCA later.

I get up, slightly bummed about being cheated out of naps for the rest of eternity, and make my way down the hall to Zahara's room. I knock, and she tells me to come in. I find her settled on her bed, brow furrowed, arms around a pillow.

"What's up?" I ask.

"One sec, I'm impregnating myself," she says, eyes squeezed shut.

"Oh…do you need me to, like…go?"

"Nope." Zahara's eyes fly open. "That should do it."

"Umm, it's not really my business, but I thought you agreed with Priyanka on the not creating more babies to fight humans thing?"

"Oh, I do," Zahara leans back into her pillows, obviously tired after creating life. "I was planning on having another right away regardless. It's not good for the first clutch to be without another clutch. They get spoiled. Young harpies are best raised in a large group with all of them pecking at and challenging each other. Also..." Zahara rubs her eyes and then levels me with an assessing look. "Also, I don't know what's going to happen with this whole Hades thing. The prophecy says we all have to sacrifice one thing. What if I lose my babies? Or my ability to have more?" Her eyes well up with tears. "I've never been afraid of battle before." She sniffs. "I guess my mother was right; children can make a woman weak."

"I don't agree," I say, thinking of my own mama and how easily she's left me behind time and time again. "I love your maternal instinct, and in the end, I think it'll make you stronger."

"Thanks, BJ." Zahara smiles. "So what's going on with you?"

I sit next to her on the bed, falling backwards onto a pillow. "Have you tried sleeping yet?"

"Figured that out, did you?"

"Yeah, I guess we don't get to."

"I don't think that's quite right," Zahara says. "I think we can, we just don't have to. Same with eating. We don't *have* to, but we *can*."

I sit straight up, suddenly alert. "If you're right, does that mean I can eat whatever I want?"

"Probably," Zahara shrugs. "I mean, you're a goddess."

I grab her face in my hands, turning her to lock eyes with me. "Zahara, I need you to be totally sure about this." She blinks, her cheeks scrunched in my hands. "Are you saying that I can eat whatever I want and never gain any weight?"

"Yeah," her smushed lips move between my hands, and I can't understand what she says next, so I let her go. "I mean, if you do gain some pounds I'm sure you can just wish it away."

I clap my hands together. "You have no idea what this means to me. ALARIC!"

My super hot boyfriend appears next to the bed, confused. "Are you alright? Brandee Jean, did something happen?"

"Yes," I say, taking his hand. "Something did. I need you to do something for me."

"Anything," he says, coming to his knees beside the bed.

"Okay, I need you to go to Culver's and get me a Butter Burger, cheese and bacon and everything, no pickle. Then I need a super size fries from McDonald's and one of those big melty salted caramel cookies from Wendy's. Oh, swing by the Brat Stop and get me a few brats with sauerkraut. The Cheese Castle is right by there, should just be a short hop for you. We should probably get a cheese tray, the one they do for Packer's games. With fifty different types of cheese. Also,

I'm going to need a large Hawaiian pizza and then one of those dessert pizzas from Godfather's, you know, with the streusel? Extra icing on that."

"Um?" Alaric looks to Zahara, who is thinking hard.

"Definitely grab some garlic sticks while you're there," she says, rubbing her midsection. "I feel some cravings coming on. Oh, and ice cream. The kind with Oreos in it."

"Oreos!" I yell, pumping my fist in the air. "Double stuff, for sure. Also, those Little Debbie chocolate cupcakes with the white loops on top."

"Oh yeah," Zahara agrees. "We're going to need at least two dozen of those."

"I'm sorry," Alaric shakes his head. "Did you call me here to do a burger run?"

"Hey," I object. "I just asked for the one burger. I also need pizza and sweets. Are you writing this down? You should be writing this down."

Alaric stands up. "BJ, I thought you needed something important. I'm not your personal Uber Eats."

"It *is* important," I say, rising to my feet to stand beside him. "I've spent my whole life not eating the things I want, because Mama said I had to. When I did sneak my favorite things— all the stuff I just told you—I got in trouble. Like, big trouble. I had to work off every calorie I took in. And now…" I spin, showing off my goddess body. "I don't have to anymore."

I take his hand in mine. "Alaric, listen. We're going to face down the head of the underworld, and there are no guarantees we get out of this alive. Cassie's prophecy said we'd all sacrifice to Hades. I've been making sacrifices my whole life, and it sounds like there are more in front of me. Let me have this, please?"

His face changes as I speak, sliding into understanding. "Okay," he says. "But I'm adding fish and chips to that list."

"That's so British of you," Zahara rolls her eyes.

"Before I go, though…" Alaric hesitates and then adds in a rush, "Am I boring?"

"Kinda," Zahara says. "It's more the steadfast and staid sort of boring if that helps."

I put my hands on my hips. "Who cares what Bex thinks, Alaric?"

His eyes narrow on me. "You're not answering the question. Why aren't you answering the question, BJ?"

I gulp. He caught me. The truth is, I agree with Zahara. Alaric is boring but in the best possible way. Besides his incredible hotness, it's one of my favorite things about him. But he clearly has a whole thing now (thanks, Bex) about being boring, so I don't feel like he'll buy my whole boring is good speech.

"You can shoot fire from your hands," I try instead. "That's not boring."

"Yes, but I almost never do it. Only that one time in the cave with you and honestly it made me very uncomfortable."

Zahara snorts and I send some stink eye her way before focusing on Alaric once more.

"You're a god! That's not boring. And you can teleport, which is amazing. None of us can do that."

"All I've done with teleportation is act as your errand boy," Alaric reminds me. "If Trevor could teleport he'd be blinking himself into the Queen's bathtub."

"Ew, really?" I wrinkle my nose in disgust. "Isn't she like, really old?"

"I mean when she's not in it!" Alaric clarifies.

"Trevor is an entertaining madman," Zahara laughs. "The first time I met him…"

"Not now, Zahara!" I screech.

Alaric shakes his head. "It's fine. I've heard it my whole life. I'm steady Alaric, and Trevor is the one everyone wants at their party." He slumps into Zahara's desk chair, which makes me think he's probably not going on my food run anytime soon. "You didn't even mention my ability to shapeshift. You've probably forgotten I can do it. I've only done it the once, because that also makes me feel very uncomfortable. It feels wrong wearing someone else's skin."

"Sure," I nod in agreement. "And your own skin is so nice, any shift is gonna be trading down."

Alaric seems to barely hear me. He's just sitting, being very quietly upset.

"You know, Alaric," Zahara says. "I sort of understand how you feel. With all the babymaking I've been doing, I feel a bit like I'm turning into my mother. It's not exactly what I expected when I set out to win the crown."

I shoot to my feet with a rumble of thunder. "You're both right! We're thinking too small! Tomorrow we fight Hades, but tonight...tonight we hit the town. ALL the towns. We're going to find an underground club and dance. Then a fight. If we can't find a fight we'll start one. Oh, and let's break into a bank vault. We won't steal anything, but I just want to roll around in piles of money. American money, please; it wouldn't feel the same having a bunch of pounds pressed against my bare ass." I stop to think for a moment, but Zahara jumps in.

"Let's invite ourselves backstage at a rock concert!"

"Oh!" Alaric jumps up, his eyes aglow. "Or crash the backstage of an opera."

Zahara and I exchange looks. The kind that says, "Let's give him this one."

"Oooh opera, always wanted to crash that," I agree with all the fake enthusiasm I can muster. "And in between," I add. "We'll eat."

21

The sun is just starting to rise as I sink into a tub full of bubbles, a Butter Burger in one hand and a cupcake the size of my face in the other.

"Is the bruising on my face going down yet?" I ask Zahara. She's hanging out by the toilet. Girl doesn't want to admit it, but she can't hold her ambrosia. I didn't even know what ambrosia was, but sometime during our crazy night we dropped in on Edie. We were having so much fun after the MMA fight (which is where my bruising came from) and playing slots in Monte Carlo, that I thought she might like to join us. But she was busy with Val. And by busy I mean getting busy.

Before ordering us to get out, Edie said if we were gonna act like a bunch of idiot gods, we should do it right—and that meant getting drunk. Apparently, ambrosia is the gods' version of a Long Island Iced Tea. She even told us where to get some. Hermes and another god own a seedy strip club in Florida. Their first one burnt down, but they rebuilt, making it bigger and sleazier. Edie figured they'd have a good stash of ambrosia and suggested we help ourselves. She also suggested we help ourselves to the safe if we needed some cash on hand. I think Hermes is on Edie's permanent shit list.

Honestly, I'm not much of a drinker. Mama always said booze was basically liquid french fries and would live on my hips 'til the day I died. Even though I don't have to count calories anymore, some habits die hard. So tonight, I focused on inhaling all the food I'd been denied and figured I'd get around to trying ambrosia another time.

Zahara, though, loved the stuff. Said it helped calm her maternal nerves. Although I gotta say she didn't seem all that calm when she threatened to tear Hermes' wings off his ankles and shove them up his ass. That's when he was shouting at us after we broke into T&A FOR 2.

He told us to get out or he'd show us what a real god could do. Zahara laughed in his face. I'd like to say that Alaric and I were there for backup, but truth is we were too busy staring at the guy with his gigantic dick sitting in a wheelbarrow. At first I thought it was some sad out of season watermelon, because he was wearing a striped sock sorta thing over his man bits. But then he saw Alaric and clearly became, ahhh, well, you know.

Alaric explained that this dude was Priapus...and yes, that was his giant penis. Sometimes bigger is definitely NOT better.

"Uuugggh," Zahara groans now. She peels off some of the Mardi Gras beads draped around her neck—a remnant from another part of our evening. Zahara flashed so many people...and then they mostly threw beads at her out of confusion. "Maybe I need more ambrosia. You know, hair of the dog and all that?"

"No more ambrosia," Alaric says, appearing out of nowhere. In his hands he has a DQ Blizzard, McDonald's french fries, and the cheese platter I asked for. I honestly didn't think he'd remember the cheese platter, but he did.

Also, wrapped around his neck is his new pet—a boa constrictor.

It took one look at Alaric and fell in love. I guess the feeling was mutual...or maybe not. He actually looked pretty squicked out at first when the boa started wrapping itself around him, but then Alaric saw his reflection in the mirror of Sting's dressing room (yes, that Sting).

"Does a boring guy wear a snake as an accessory?" He didn't wait for an answer before shouting, "He certainly does not."

Later he also insisted on a tattoo that said, BOA MAN. Zahara and I could not talk him out of it, though we did at least convince him to have it inked on a part of his body where the sun doesn't tend to shine.

Now, Alaric hands me fries. Tossing what's left of the cupcake over my shoulder, I grab for them with two hands. He leans down to kiss me, then snags one of my fries. I gotta admit, he looks super hot and mysterious in his Phantom of the Opera costume. He's even wearing the white face mask.

We tried the real opera, but after five minutes I was like, aw hell no. So we compromised and went Broadway instead. Giggling, I sink further into the tub, remembering Alaric dressed in the phantom costume and me in one of my Tata's Tops tube tops (Mama looked so good in hers that I wanted one too) waltzing across the stage. I mean, sorta waltzing. Alaric knows how, but I sure don't. Then, so Zahara didn't feel left out, he waltzed her back the other way. She did better, 'cause she just levitated and let Alaric lead.

Gently, Alaric's fingers trace the bruising left on my cheek. "Maybe you shouldn't have insisted that you take on five guys at once," he says.

"Probably not," I agree. "But I still won."

Alaric leans down to give me a long lingering kiss. If it wasn't for the snake in my face, it'd be the best of my life.

"Pardon me." A stiff butler-type guy enters the bathroom He keeps his eyes on the ceiling so he's not ogling us, which I gotta admit is pretty classy. "The Queen would like to know when she can expect to have her bath back?"

"Oh crap," Zahara says, shooting to her feet. "We got that council meeting in like thirty minutes."

"But I still have to finish my Butter Burger!"

"We'll bring it with us, BJ," Alaric says. Turning to the butler, he adds, "Tell the Queen we appreciate her patience."

"Quite," Butler guy replies, which I think is snooty British for 'Go bugger yourself.'

"All right, time to go." Alaric grabs one of Zahara's talons and then reaches for my hand.

"Wait!" I cry. "I'm—"

In the blink of an eye, we're back in my room. Or at least Alaric and I are.

I'm dripping wet and naked, but right now I'm more concerned that Zahara was left in the Queen's bathroom.

"Did you forget Zahara?" I ask as Alaric pulls off his Phantom cloak and wraps it around my shoulders.

"Zahara is fine. She's in her own suite. And Sting is in my own suite."

"You named the snake Sting? I like it." I smile and take a step closer to Alaric. "But what are you doing here?"

Reaching out, he grabs me and pulls me close so we're pressed together in all the places that matter. "I'm proving to you that I'm not boring or steady or steadfast."

I frown. "Alaric, I like steady and steadfast. It's nice knowing you'll never leave me high and dry like…" I pause the words sticking in my throat. "Like my Mama did."

He kisses me gently on the forehead. "I will never leave you high and dry. Or…" His hands find my bare skin beneath his cloak. "Wet and bubbly."

The words are just what I needed to hear. I melt into him and we stumble toward the bed.

Suddenly, though, I remember, "Alaric! Didn't Zahara say the council meeting was soon?"

"Let them wait. We're gods now, remember?" He grins at me and for a moment he is a total bad boy. Then the smile fades and he becomes my slightly boring Alaric once more as he adds, "Although making them wait more than ten minutes would be unforgivably rude."

I can't help but laugh as love and affection floods through me.

"Don't worry, we'll have a Wisconsin quickie."

"What's that?"

Now it's my turn to grin as I flip Alaric so he's face up on my mattress and I'm on top straddling him.

"Let me show you."

22

Alaric and I get to the meeting just in time to catch the end of Athena's lecture. She was telling Zahara off for last night's shenanigans and how this is the type of nonsense that brought Zeus down and without discipline we'll find ourselves in the same place as him.

Athena's nostrils flare as Alaric and I slip into our seats. He made sure to stop and retrieve Sting, who he was worried might be missing him.

"Now that you two have finally deigned to bestow some of your precious time on the rest of us, we can get started." Athena looks down at her watch. "Except that it's time for my daily tea and tonic. Let's take ten, everyone." With that she sweeps from the room, apparently unaware or uninterested in the irony of her telling of us off for wasting time and then doing the exact same thing herself.

I lean into Zahara and whisper, "Sorry. Alaric and I were…"

Zahara cuts me off with a glare. "We all know what you and Alaric were doing. Just next time don't leave me alone to deal with Athena's lecture. Okay?"

"Sorry," I give her arm a squeeze. "Was there any part of last night she was extra upset about?"

Zahara shrugs. "She mentioned us recreating the running of the bulls with Alaric shapeshifting into the bull." Lowering her voice, she leans closer and adds, "I don't think she knows about Alaric transporting us up to the space station, so let's keep that one sealed tight, yeah?"

I nod, and then turn as Edie's hand lands on my shoulder.

"BJ, this is Fern. She's a witch and a healer, one of my good friends from Mount Olympus Academy. I brought her here because I thought she might have some ideas about how we can defeat Hades."

"I think you met my girlfriend, Marguerite?" Fern smiles.

"Oh, yeah. She helped save our asses. What is it with you guys and dating vamps?" I ask her and Edie.

The girl gets a sly smile and is about to speak, but first Alaric stands up. "Before you continue," he says, "I'd first like to ask if this is even possible? Hades is a god, the god of the underworld."

"Yes," Edie says. "But it is possible to defeat them. Hades is a god, and a scary one, too. But I killed Zeus—the most powerful god."

"Well…you kind of killed him," Zahara says. "I had to finish him off."

"Fair point; it isn't easy to kill a god," Edie nods. "Zeus had all the powers in the world, but there was a weapon that could kill him. I found it and then met Zeus in battle. It was difficult, but it wasn't impossible. Hades isn't as powerful as you think. He has zombies and minions that do his work for him so that he never has to put himself in harm's way."

"And remember," I say, touching Alaric's hand. "Between the three of us we have Zeus' powers. We can do this." Maybe three really is the magic number.

"The real problem," Fern says, "is similar to what we faced

with Mr. Zee…sorry, Zeus. There was a weapon that could defeat him, but we had to get it in order to effectively neuter him. Like Edie said, Hades has many powers, but his biggest weapon is the ability to raise the dead."

"Also throw fireballs," Bex pipes up from across the table. "I took the liberty of doing some research last night and came across that interesting tidbit."

Alaric leans into me and whispers into my ear, "She was at the library last night. Who's boring now?"

I push the snake out of my hair and give Alaric's cheek a little kiss. "Not you, babe."

"Fireballs can cause significant harm," Fern acknowledges, "but the greatest threat is the zombie horde. The dead will do as he says. If we can take that power away from him, he is much less of a threat. He'll have no undead army. With the help of my fellow witches and Priya's coven, we have created a magical collar that, once snapped around his neck, interrupts his ability to use his powers."

She snaps her fingers.

"Then what happens to the zombies?" I ask. "Do they die? I mean, they're already dead."

Fern shakes her head. "The zombies may drop in their tracks and return to being corpses. They may poof out of existence. They may become decent hard-working members of society. I just don't know. This is an experiment that's never before been attempted."

Beside me, Zahara shifts uncomfortably. "I'm willing to give it a go," she says. "Except for the whole part about getting close enough to the god of the dead to snap a collar around his neck. That seems like a stretch."

Fern nods. "I know, and I'm sorry. It's the best I could come up with on short notice."

"Do you think you could possibly maybe pretty please make the collar not let him shoot fireballs, too?" I ask. The

Butter Burger (and pizza and fries and big melty cookie) are turning uncomfortably in my stomach at the thought.

Fern shakes her head. "That's a physical component of Hades' abilities," she says. "All I can do is interrupt his magical elements."

Athena re-enters the room and clears her throat. "I see you've begun the discussion without me. Aren't we suddenly impatient." Lilliana stands and quickly recaps everything that's been discussed. When she's finished Athena nods. "It seems I entered at the right time. The answer for how to contain Hades is simple. Cut his hands off. Then he can't throw anything."

"Wow. Harsh," I say.

She shrugs. "It's war. My uncle deserves no mercy."

"If we could maybe not mutilate anybody, that would be great," I say, scanning the council to see if anybody has any other ideas. "Also, we'd still have to get close to cut his hands off."

"How many gods are on our side?" Alaric asks Athena. "We can't plan an attack without knowing our numbers."

She tilts her head. "I don't see how that is relevant."

"How is it not?" I ask, confused. "We have Zahara, Alaric, and me as the three-in-one god. But we're newbies. Even with all this power we're going to have a hard time facing off against Hades. We need seasoned veterans... What? Why are you looking at me like that?"

"The gods don't actually fight," Zahara explains. "They get their cronies to do that for them. That's why the monsters revolted. They were sick of dying for their causes."

"But..." I look at Athena and Artemis. "You're the god of strategy, and you're the god of hunting. You're basically two bad bitches. You're not going to fight?"

Athena shakes her head. "No." At least Artemis looks a little ashamed.

"You will send the Amazons in your stead to die for you?" Alaric asks.

"They are my fighting force. I will not break millenia of tradition," Athena says.

"Some things are going to change around here," I say, fuming that she had the nerve to lecture us about having fun last night when we're getting ready to face down Hades. While she meanwhile won't even sacrifice her tea and tonic time for a council meeting!

"Preach!" Zahara adds.

"We shall see, little godling. But now, let's work with what we have," Athena says.

"I will fight by your side, and I will bring as many as I can against the zombie horde," Edie tells us. "But taking care of Hades will be up to you."

"The collar," Alaric reminds us.

Zahara asks, "How do we get that close?"

"We set a trap," Alaric says. "Trevor heard Cassie's prophecy, remember? She said that each of us would sacrifice to the one. He would have repeated that to Hades by now, quite gleefully, I'm sure. They don't only want us to fail, they're *expecting* us to. The fact that we willingly split Zeus' power between the three of us has blown Hades' mind. He thinks it makes us weaker."

"He's totally wrong," I say. "It doesn't make us weaker, it makes us stronger. I see what you're saying. He'll never even consider that we might win. He thinks we'll give in to him, and Cassie's prophecy only reinforces that."

"Not necessarily," Zahara speaks up. "A prophecy can be interpreted many different ways."

"Right," I say. "But he's going to like the part about all of us sacrificing to him, and he's going to think it means that we surrender to him. So...let's do it."

"What?" Artemis comes to her feet, cheeks red with anger.

"Let's *say* we surrender," I say. "We'll tell Hades we want to bow to him, that we want to bend the knee and prevent further bloodshed. We'll set up a meeting place and one of us will snap the collar on him."

Athena shakes her head. "It won't be that easy."

"I know," I say. "But it's the best idea we've got." I look around the table to see heads shaking in unison. Everyone looks concerned, but they're also in agreement.

"Okay," I let out a big breath. It smells like onions. I quickly wish it away and try again, this time getting something more like strawberries and cream. Nice. I can get into this goddess thing.

"Alaric," I say, turning to my boyfriend and letting him get the full blast of my sexy breath. "Can you get the message to Trevor that we'd like to set up a meeting?"

"No," Edie shakes her head. "He actually can't. If Hades is at Underworld Academy you can't go down there unless you're already dead, or have his permission, and he's not going to be giving out day passes to just anyone. We could send Marguerite or Val. As vampires, they are technically dead-ish—"

She's interrupted by a horrible crash. The ground shakes underneath us and we all grab the table for support, as dust tumbles down from the ceiling. I glance out the window to see that another hellmouth has opened, and my mother is climbing up out of it.

"A hellmouth did not just open up on my island," Athena says, crossing her arms. "Hades has gone too far."

"This is where you draw the line?" I mutter.

Mama strolls into the war room through a crack that opened in the wall, leaving a smear behind her. Her new body has already got some wear and tear on it, but her breasts are as perky as ever. As Mama always said, "God bless the man who invented silicone."

"You filthy zombie!" Athena screams. "How dare you—"

"Chill out, Wonder Woman," Mama says, barely glancing at the goddess. "I'm here to see my daughter, and I'll close the portal behind me when I leave."

"And what about the mess!" Athena demands, pointing at the crack in the ceiling, the opening in the wall, and the plaster that has rained down everywhere.

"Bill your insurance," Mama shrugs, then turns to me. "Baby! Have you put on weight?"

I grab my midsection instantly, shooting Zahara a dark look. But she shakes her head. "You haven't gained an ounce. She's trying to get to you."

I straighten up, and glare down at the corpse that used to be my mama. "I haven't gained weight, Mama. And even if I did, you know what? I don't care."

That stops her in her tracks. Her dead, squishy, stinky tracks.

"Honey," she says, one hand going to her chest in shock. "You've got to learn how to take care of yourself when you're young. Developing good eating habits now means that you won't gain weight later, like me."

She twirls, showing off what's left of her hot bod. And I've got to admit, she's still rocking it, for being dead and half-rotted.

"Mama," I say, clearing my head. "That body wasn't yours to begin with. It's at least ten years younger than you."

"BJ, I'm warning you," she says, like she always does when I get sassy.

I tilt up my chin. "And I want you to know that this morning I ate a Butter Burger with bacon."

She stops, staring at me. "You did *what*?"

"And a super size fry," I say. She flinches. "And a row of Double Stuffed Oreos." She takes a step back.

"And like twenty Little Debbies," Zahara adds, and Mama actually swoons. She's on the ground now, holding her head, her rotting locks hanging on either side of her face.

"Oh my poor, sweet girl…what have they done to you?"

"Nothing," I tell her. "They didn't do anything to me. I just decided I was going to do what I wanted. And I wanted to pig out."

"We looked at it as a kind of last meal," Alaric says, nudging me.

"That's right," I say, getting to the point. "Mama, we've decided that you're right. We are just baby gods, and don't know how to handle our full powers. We'll never stand a chance against Hades and his zombie hordes. If he will agree not to harm us, we will bend the knee and hand over our powers. On the condition that none of us, or our people, will be harmed. Can you pass that message along?"

"Yes!" Mama is back on her feet immediately. "Baby, I'm so glad you've seen the light. And don't worry about that bingeing thing. It happens. I'll tell Hades to get you one of those nice Peloton bikes once you're human again and we'll work all of that flab right off you."

I stiffen, but Alaric puts his hand on my back to remind me to stick to the plan.

"Thank you for delivering our message," I say.

Mama slips back out through the crack in the wall. One of her toes gets caught and she has to shake it loose, leaving it behind. We all watch through the window as she goes to the edge of the hellmouth. She's not like Trevor, who had private swimming lessons and his own indoor pool. She can't do a swan dive, even though she made certain I could. She settles for a cannonball, and the hellmouth closes behind her.

23

A zombie arrives with the time and location of our surrender.

"No," Zahara shakes her head. "Tell him it has to be somewhere else."

"If we're going to pull off this bluff, we can't start making demands," Alaric says. "If Hades wants to meet at my family manor, then that's where we must go. He fancies it his new base of operations."

"We'll get your eggs, and Cassie, out of there before the fighting starts," I say.

Zahara bristles. "If one feather is harmed on the head of any of my offspring…"

"I wish I could promise they'll be okay," I say. "But I don't know what will happen. Maybe we should change the location. Make it the desert or Timbuktu or…"

"No," Zahara says, sighing. "Alaric is right. If Hades catches even a whiff of a trap, he'll bolt. We'll keep it at the mansion."

We task Lilliana with a small force to protect the eggs, and Cassie. Alaric will teleport me and Zahara there, then the

Amazon force will follow through the London portal. It will take them a bit longer to get there, but hopefully also give us the element of surprise.

Fern brings the collar to us. "It closes like this," she says, demonstrating. "Once it is around Hades' neck, only the powers of Zeus can remove it."

Alaric reaches out a hand, but as soon as he touches the collar his skin sizzles. He pulls back and shies away.

"What was that?" I ask.

Fern studies him. "I was unaware that you were fae."

Alaric sighs. "It's not something that I like to share."

"The collar is iron, infused with magic and ancient spells, but iron nonetheless. Alaric will not be able to touch it."

"Great," Zahara says. "That means that only BJ or myself can do the dirty work."

"I will be there, fighting," Alaric says.

"We all will. Together," I tell them.

Zahara takes the collar. "You two must distract him and I will try to fasten this around his neck. Perhaps he will not ever imagine that a lowly monster will be his downfall."

"That would be his mistake," I tell her.

"Yes," she agrees. "Sometimes being underestimated is a gift."

"The Amazons are ready," Athena tells us. "Gods speed, you three."

Alaric puts a hand on each of our shoulders and we are once again on the manicured lawn of his manor house.

"Oh, gods," Alaric says. "What did Hades do to the gardens?"

Instead of a beautiful, stately, country garden there's a hellscape of burned earth and rotting undead zombies. Hades has fashioned a throne for himself out of skeletons; flames engulf it, the red of hellfire. The skulls open and scream their turmoil. Trevor stands on one side of the grisly throne and my mother on the other. The hellmouth is a gaping wound behind them.

"You have come to bend the knee!" Hades booms. "I knew that I would be king of the gods, even as my brother, Zeus, tried to reclaim his powers. What a fool! Letting two teenagers and a monster defeat him!" He spits out the word monster like it's a maggoty turd.

"You are correct," Alaric says, and adds after I nudge him with my elbow, "Oh great and powerful Hades."

Trevor raises an eyebrow at Alaric's words. My mother rubs Hades' shoulder.

"Zeus was nothing, in the end," Alaric continues. "But you, you've proven yourself to be a true king. We will offer our powers to you..." Behind Hades, in the sky, a figure passes in front of a cloud. A dragon-shaped shadow. Edie and the Amazons are here.

I give Alaric the tip of my elbow once more, just to make sure he sees them too. Then I add, "Please, let us gift you our swords, a representation of the power we hold. When they are in your hands, you should receive the power of Zeus."

We stand, moving in unison, like we planned. My stomach tightens and I try to stop my trembling by repeating to myself, *I am a goddess. I am a goddess. I am a goddess.*

The plan is for me and Alaric to stab him while Zahara fastens the collar.

Before we can take another step closer, it becomes apparent that my sword skills aren't going to be put to the test. At least not yet.

"No!" Hades booms. "I am not a fool like my brother. I will not underestimate you. Hand over your swords one at a time."

Alaric and I freeze, but Zahara takes a step forward. I want to grab her shirt and pull her back, while another part of me wants to cheer her on. Mostly, though, I'm so glad she's on my team.

I hold my breath as she gets a little closer. Zahara is smart enough to have done the calculations. She must know exactly how fast she needs to be in order to bend the knee, deliver the sword, and snap the collar on before Hades knows what hit him.

But my hopes fade as I see Hades sneer at Zahara's approach.

"Monster, do you think to go first?" Hades asks. "Disgusting." His fiery eyes fall on me. "You, pretty girl. You surrender first, and perhaps I will trade in your mother for the younger, prettier version."

My mother drops her hand from his shoulder and her look is half sad, half angry. It's one I've seen before. When you're the type of person who's attracted to bottom of the barrel boyfriends, you're also gonna end up being the person who watches those same sluggos hit on your teenage daughter. I'll say this for Mama, though, she never stood for it.

It didn't matter how much she liked a guy. If his eyes lingered on my backside too long or if he made a remark about my tight ass or—worse yet—if he just reached out and gave my buttocks a squeeze, well then that was it.

The leer got him a slap upside the head and Mama pointing him to the door. The remark meant Mama went after him with the broom. I'm pretty sure it's the only reason we owned a broom, 'cause Mama wasn't much for sweeping up any dirtballs that weren't living. And finally, the one man who dared to put his hands on me got Mama throwing knives at him. She had some wicked good aim too. Later, after the police had taken our statements and left, Mama confessed knife throwing had been her talent back when she was a pageant girl. When I asked why she hadn't passed that talent down to me, Mama said, "Never choose a talent that scares the shit out of everyone."

But like a lot of things Mama once said, I'm taking it with a grain of salt now. Because I've got some new talents that are pretty darn scary, but Hades is definitely not quaking in his boots.

And beside him, Mama doesn't have a broom or knives or anything else out. I get it. When she chased those old boyfriends out, she was giving up sex and companionship and the hope of a man who'd take her one of those all-you-can-drink Caribbean cruises. Really, just the things every girl dreams of.

But now there's way more on the line. Her body. Her life.

"Baby, never let a man control you," Mama always said. "No matter what happens in a relationship, I got my house, I got my life. If things go south, I got no problem telling any man to eat shit and die."

But Mama's not saying anything to Hades now. Even as she watches him trying to undress me with his eyes.

Tears press at the corners of my eyeballs, but no way am I gonna let them flow. I'm done crying for Mama and her bad choices. I'm done being let down.

Also, if we do defeat Hades I'm sure there'll be some sort of commemorative photo and I don't want to be all puffy-faced for it.

"Come sit on Papa Hades' knees, pretty girl," he croons, a long finger with a blackened nail beckoning me.

I inch forward, trying to stall for time, letting the Amazons get into position.

"You'd really take me?" I ask. "After all this?" The words are heavy in my mouth but I say them anyway.

"I might be...convinced." Hades leers at me. "There must be a reason you're called BJ." He laughs and I hazard a glance at my mother.

Her eyes meet mine. "Just do as he says, baby," Mama encourages in a quiet voice. It almost sounds like she's fighting tears too. I just out my chin to keep it from trembling and step forward. "Hades, I offer you my powers," I say, holding up my sword.

He reaches out a hand but before he can grab the sword I swing it around and stab it into his neck. "For you to choke on."

He stands, growing taller, his rage enhancing his stature. I hold on as long as I can, but my feet are soon dangling as I grip the sword, and he bats me aside, the sword still embedded in his neck.

Alaric teleports to my side, pulling me to my feet. Hades roars, and Alaric steps in front me, arms spread wide in protection.

"You thought to double cross me?" Hades yells. "You can't kill me. I am the god of death."

He looks past us, to the house. "I had so coveted your earthly riches," he says. "I made my academy one of delights and pleasures. A place for all the dead to feel alive again. But you are just humans, and living ones, at that. You do not deserve what I offer."

There's a horrible crack, and behind us, the manor house begins to sink into the ground, flames licking at it as it tilts crazily.

"My babies!" Zahara screams, instinctively running towards the now fire-engulfed structure. Alaric grabs her around the waist, preventing her from taking flight.

"It's too late!" he yells at her. "You'll only be hurt!"

"That's my family!" she screeches at him, talons slashing at his face.

"I know," Alaric says, grabbing her wrists and pinning them to her side. "Mine is in there, too."

"No!" Trevor shouts, grabbing at Hades, who has shrunk

back to normal size, and pulled my sword from his neck. The wound begins to close. "You promised!"

Hades backhands him and he flies through the air and falls to the ground. "Silence! Touch me again and I'll send the rotting flesh I gave you back to the ground."

Out of the corner of my eye I see a group of Amazons, led by Lilliana, climbing out of the hellmouth hole. Lilliana has Cassie slung over her shoulder, and each of her soldiers is carrying a harpy chick, their bald, peaky heads bobbing with each step.

Zahara stops struggling in Alaric's arms when she spots them. He follows her gaze, his face at first hopeful, but then falling. There is no sign of his parents.

"You imbeciles!" Hades shouts. "Do you really think you can win against the god of the dead? My army is legion!"

Hades raises his hands and thousands of zombies pour from the hellmouth. Other creatures follow; things I've never heard of, and thankfully, have never seen before. There are demons that scurry on the ground like spiders while winged devils fly through the air. Mama immediately drops, arms protecting her hair.

Shit. Plan A was for Zahara to clap the collar onto Hades. I improvised a Plan B by stabbing him in the neck, which only got us into this mess.

Time for Plan C...too bad I don't know what that is.

Arrows shoot through the air as the Amazons arrive, their trip on foot from the London portal slowing them down. They're welcome, even if they're a little late. Edie swoops down in dragon form and picks up several of the undead in her arms, throwing them to knock down the others, then lights the whole wriggling mass on fire. Her vampire boyfriend and his friends are here now, too, using their freakish vampire strength to tear heads from undead bodies.

"Zahara, now!" I shout. She shoots through the air above

my head, hands out, collar ready. She's closing in on Hades, who is watching with bloodlust while one of his zombies screeches as Edie tears him in half. I shudder. He doesn't even care that one of his own has gone down; he just loves that it's violent.

But the wind is slipping through Zahara's wings as she closes in on her prey, and Hades spins. He releases a fireball, and she's knocked from the sky, engulfed in flames.

"No!" I scream and run to her side.

She's a smoking mess of charred skin, but I can see the lower layers of muscle and tendon re-knitting themselves even as I hover over her. On her back, the bony nubs of her wings are attempting to send out fibrous threads, but they fail to catch onto each other. Her body must decide it's more important to keep her alive, because the last few strands fall, losing their glow, from the bony nubs at her back.

"Zahara!" I cry, leaning over her. "You've lost your wings!"

"I'll live," she tells me, shoving the collar into my hands. "Finish this!"

Alaric is at my side and he yells, "I'll cover you."

We make our way through the mass of zombies and fighting Amazons. Val, the vampire to our left, is under a mountain of the undead. Edie lands beside him and burns the zombies to ash. Val gives her a quick nod of appreciation and rises to his feet, steam coming from his surprisingly unsinged shoulders.

In the sky, winged demons are being taken out by arrows and miniature harpies. It's Zahara's children, I realize. Wow, they really do grow up so fast. It seems like just yesterday—actually, I guess it *was* yesterday—she was laying her eggs and now they're fighting an army of the dead. Battle must be instinctual for harpies, because they're fierce, attacking with tooth and claw, and make sure to keep the flying devils off our backs. Their tiny squeaks of triumph must reach their mother's ears because I hear her cheering them on, shouting advice on when to dive and when to wheel.

"You may have taken my wings, but the joke's on you, asshole!" Zahara yells, vaulting up into the air, even though she's wingless. "I got the ability to fly!"

I watch, open mouthed, as she swoops and gathers her children to her, rallying them for another charge.

"BJ! Watch out!" Alaric knocks me to the side, and I rise to my feet, sputtering, to see a new demon rising from the depths of hell. It has no head, just a chest made of circular teeth. It has no eyes to see, but still seems to know exactly where we are.

Alaric's grip tightens on my arm. "An anthropophagus," he says.

"A whatey a whatsit?" I ask, but then decide I'm less interested in what to call it than I am in killing it. I shoot lightning at it and Alaric teleports us out of the way, but the creature anticipates our moves.

Can I heal if I am devoured whole? I wonder.

Then a figure appears between us, wielding a knife and sword. Artemis slashes at the demon, taking off one leg and throwing it off balance.

"You came!" I cry out, grateful. She broke with thousands of years of tradition to help us.

"Can't let you have all the fun," she tells us with a wink. "But if any of the other gods ask, I was just passing through on the way to my skiing holiday. I saw this beastie and couldn't resist putting my mark on it." She tosses her knife my way and I duck instinctively. Artemis laughs, not unkindly. "Pick up the knife and finish the job!"

Alaric nods and we teleport to Hades' throne. Hades snatches at me, but Alaric throws himself in front of me.

"Augh!" Alaric screams as Hades' hand closes around his shoulder, driving him down to his knees.

"One down, two to go," Hades laughs.

"Alaric!" I rush to his rescue, but someone grabs my arm. It's Trevor.

"I've got the girl, master," Trevor says. "Take Alaric's powers but don't destroy him, resurrect my home, and she's yours."

I give him a jolt and he lets go of me, shrieking.

I'm tempted to give Trevor a few more zaps...but for once he actually sorta stuck up for Alaric. In his own Trevor sort of way. Which is more than my mama's done for me.

Shoving Trevor aside, I call up all my strength and launch myself at Hades. Alaric falls from his grasp and then it's just me and Hades grappling on the ground.

I go for his eyes, but he anticipates me and grabs my hands. With one squeeze the bones in my hand crunch, breaking.

I howl, the pain unbelievable.

Hades grins. "Good thing your name's BJ and not handjob."

I kick him in the balls with enough force to make his nuts come out the next time he blows his nose.

It definitely takes the air out of him. Alaric appears and teleports me out of Hades' reach before he can recover.

"Where are you going?" Hades roars at me. "We were just starting to have some fun. Get back over here and hand over your power. NOW. Or your mother will die. Again." I spin back to face him, and see that he has his hand around her neck. "I can pop off her head like a bottle cap."

"Mama!" I cry, dropping to my knees. I can't do this alone. I'm only one third of a god.

I stretch one of my broken hands out toward her, the bones knitting themselves together is nearly as painful as them breaking apart.

My mother looks at me, and even though it's a two-dollar-stripper's face, it's all Mama in her eyes

"BJ, baby…" She pauses. "You be the Queen you were always meant to be. Remember what all I taught you. Tits high. Ass out. And always—" Like a snake striking, Mama reaches out one manicured hand and drives a lacquered nail deep into Hades' left eye. "Eat shit and die!" comes the guttural yell.

He wails in pain, and his hand convulsively snaps Mama's neck. I watch her head roll off to the side, and I think she might be smiling.

"Now, BJ!" someone yells, and I snap into motion, running to Hades' side, where he had thrown my sword after pulling it from his neck.

Knowing Mama sacrificed herself for me, I grab it, and drive it in between his ribs. There's no time to second guess it or feel queasy. My poor hands, though, protest as I squeeze the hilt tight.

"My Mama always said," I say to Hades between teeth gritted tight against the pain, wanting his attention on me as Alaric comes running in on his other side. Alaric's sword slides into Hades, running him through so our blades meet in the middle. We've got Hades skewered like a shrimp on a stick.

And he knows it. "You little bitch," he snarls.

"Naw," I answer, faking cheerfulness. "That's not what Mama used to say."

I'd love to be the one to snap the collar around Hades' neck, but he's still much taller than me, and I can't reach his neck. He struggles even as black blood gurgles from his mouth. I know Alaric and I won't be able to hold him for much longer.

"Zahara!" I shout.

She zips down and I toss her the collar. Or I try, but my

hand opens too late and it bobbles, hitting the ground and then skittering beyond my reach. Zahara dives for it, but Trevor gets there first. His fist closes around the iron collar, and his face constricts with pain.

"It's iron!" Alaric shouts at his brother, who is also half-fae. But Trevor won't let go of it, despite the obvious torture.

"Toss that trickery into the hellmouth, boy," Hades calls to him.

Trevor looks up at Hades and smiles through clenched teeth. "This, I think, is the point where I cut my losses." With a flip of his wrist, he sends the collar flying toward Zahara who neatly catches it.

Hades snaps his fingers and just like that—Trevor dissolves into dust.

"No, brother!" Alaric cries, while at the same time, Hades rears back wildly.

Distracted by Trevor's death and Alaric's pain at witnessing his brother die a second time, my sword slips free. I land on my ass as Hades spins to face Alaric. I heft my sword overhead, ready to drive it into Hades again. But Zahara's talons dig into his shoulder as she lands. Alaric teleports away before Hades can smash him to bits. He wheels on me again. My hands cramp up, probably the last of the broken bones healing, and my sword clatters to the ground at my feet.

A rumble of laughter comes from Hades' throat…

And then Zahara snaps the collar closed around his neck.

It clicks with a sonic blast that shoots through the battlefield, knocking everyone down. The zombie army lay where they fell, now only rotting corpses without the power of Hades animating them. There is a cheer from the Amazons.

A hot whirlwind appears over the hellmouth sucking in demons and the rest of Hades' army. They scratch and scramble at the edges of the hellmouth, but without Hades' power holding it open, it collapses on itself.

"No!!!" Hades yells, tumbling to his knees, now a normal sized man. The last of his army disappears with a *pop* as the hellmouth closes.

The victorious cheer that follows is deafening.

24

"In closing, I'd like to thank Zahara's children, Artemis, our vampire friends, Edie, and..."

I try to stifle a yawn as Bex rambles on. She'd said "in closing" but she's still got at least five sheets of paper left in this speech. She's super well spoken, and technically, I don't have to yawn—just like I don't have to eat or sleep—but I'm just bitchy enough to go ahead and do it anyway.

Bex sees it, as I intended her to. She's filled a hole that's been missing in my life since the end of my pageant days— the frenemy.

Now she raises a perfect eyebrow, and then launches into the part of the speech where she details what we've accomplished with Underworld Academy, now renamed Underworld Reformatory.

Under the table, Alaric's hand finds mine and he squeezes my fingers. I squeeze back in acknowledgement.

Just as Cassie said, we all ended up sacrificing something to Hades. Zahara lost her wings, I lost Mama, and Alaric lost his ancestral home, his parents trapped inside as it descended to the underworld.

My mind drifts as I remember the mess of the battlefield, and the scorching heat of Edie's dragon fire as she disposed of the zombies—now only bodies—by cremation. I carried Mama's head to the pyre, but without a tear in my eye. I didn't know this woman; my Mama's spirit had left this body and the one before that. Hopefully for something better.

I clutch Alaric's hand in mine, remembering the one thing we didn't find—Trevor's body. Not even the tiniest little scrap left. When Hades poofed him to dust, he was thorough. Alaric doesn't really believe that Trevor was trying to help us defeat Hades when he tossed the collar to Zahara. He thinks Trevor was just sick of slowly rotting away. He did stink at the end—and I mean according to my nose, not my moral compass.

I didn't argue with Alaric about Trevor's motivations, which seem to be permanently lost with him. But to be honest, I don't know.

Someone yelled at me, urging me forward to attack Hades at just the right moment. At the time, I was sure it was Alaric. But now I'm not so sure. I don't have to sleep, but I still do, and my goddess dreams are much more detailed than my regular old human dreams were. I remember everything in perfect detail, and I'm positive it was Trevor who told me to take Hades out.

But Alaric has had enough to deal with, having lost his parents. I haven't mentioned Trevor's last minute team switch to anyone.

"In closing—"

"Again," I mutter into Alaric's neck, and he shushes me.

"*In closing,*" Bex repeats. "I'd like to invite the council on a tour of Underworld Reformatory, to be followed by a reception."

A concerned murmur rises from the circular table, but Bex only smiles. "As you know, Hades was our first inmate.

Since then, we've been using the Amazons to round up the bad paranormals. The cells and grounds are well guarded by Zahara's children. The Paranormal Patrols are constantly adding more inmates to the population, and the humans have been mollified by this step on our part. Overall, Underworld Reformatory has been an unparalleled success."

"For now," Zahara whispers to me. "Putting that many baddies together is asking for trouble."

"It's the best we've got," I say. "And I have faith in your brood. They'll keep everyone in line."

Zahara only shrugs. "We're just putting off the problem for a later time," she says. "Mark my words."

I rise along with Alaric to follow the rest of the council to a portal that Athena has opened for us to pass through on this day jaunt to jail. One of Zahara's first born—full grown now—stands at the entrance to the portal, handing out glowing bracelets. With her is a teen boy, smallish but cute in a mega dork kinda way. He is introduced as the Warden...Greg. That's how they roll in UWR.

Greg welcomes us and explains the bracelets.

"For the living," he says, sliding it onto my wrist. "Visitors to the underworld who want to return must wear these at all times."

"Ugh...I got yellow.," I say, shaking my new bangle. "What's yours?"

"Pink," Alaric says, holding up his wrist.

"Oh! Tradesies?" I ask, but he shakes his head. "I don't think these are made to come off."

I inspect mine more closely, to find that it's not exactly touching my wrist. It hovers an inch above it on all sides, immobile.

We're pushed forward and soon we're in a dark hall, our wristbands lighting the way.

"Devil's Dorm," Greg says, acting as our tour guide. "Or,

as we call it, Cell Block D. We keep high level prisoners of interest down here. We're thinking of starting a program for inmates to help in the world of the living...but it's early stages. We have some really unique pieces of work in this block, and I mean that both mentally and physically. There are some very curious cross-species here; what we would call a *Moggy* back at Mount Olympus Academy. Some of them require special attention in order to retain them.

"A Moggy?" I ask, the word catching my attention.

"Yes," Greg says, nodding. "For example, we have a fae down here who was also a zombie at one point. When Hades was defeated, the zombie's physical bodies were no longer animated. They were "dead," for lack of a better word in relation to the zombie life cycle. However, because his fae blood could not be entirely extinguished, he entered a new phase of life as a shade."

"Oh?" I'm instantly curious. "Like at Bed, Bath and Beyond? What a boring life."

Greg laughs. "No, a shade as in he's a ghost now. The ghost of a fae...which means that incarcerating him was particularly difficult. As a fae, iron can be used as a form of containment, but he's also a ghost, and doesn't have a physical body."

"So, regular bars don't work because he can walk through walls?"

"Precisely," Greg nods. "So we had to put him in a room that was reinforced with iron bearings in the walls. He may be a ghost, but he's still fae; he can't stand the touch of iron."

"Wow, I say. "This all sounds super complicated."

"Sometime I'll tell you about how to contain a vampire minotaur who is also partially an angel, and has multiple personality disorder. Whew," Greg shakes his head. "That was a tough one."

The Devils' Dorm was one of the first buildings erected

for Underworld Academy, forged directly from the iron of the earth. As such, it's the perfect place to harbor fae who have defied the laws against hurting humans."

"Are you okay?" I spin, concerned for Alaric, but he seems fine.

"Something in my band," I think, he says, holding it up for me to say that it's changed from a soft pink to a bright red. "It's protecting me, absorbing the power of the iron."

"Huh…I wonder what mine does?" I shake my wrist, but it remains immobile. And a pretty boring yellow. "Like, maybe it's not letting the humidity get to my hair, or something," I say.

"Your hair *is* on point," a voice cuts through the dank hallway. "Being a goddess clearly agrees with you."

"What?" I yell. I've gotten pretty accustomed to being a goddess, and having people pay me compliments most of the day. But there's a slight mocking edge to this compliment. And I feel like I know that voice too…

I take a step closer as she continues. "Please, help me, BJ. They locked me up with these miscreants, but I'm innocent, I swear."

"Shauna?" I stare at my old friend. After all that time I spent looking for her, here she is in the last place I expected her.

Behind her, a pair of gossamer wings flickers, electric blue. I can't help but be transfixed.

"Like them?" she asks. "Sorry I couldn't share before, but I just didn't know who I could trust."

Ever since our conversation with that biker, I'd been thinking that my whole friendship with Shauna was just an illusion. That she'd suckered me.

But now seeing her again, I'm just so happy she's still in one piece. I don't care about the wings or the lies.

I rush toward her. "Shauna, I'm so sorry. I felt so bad when you were taken—"

A bat comes out of nowhere, dive-bombing me and screeching. Swatting at it, I stumble back until I bump into Alaric.

In the blink of an eye, the bat shifts into Greg. He is disheveled and out of breath, as he huffs, "Don't get any closer to her. She's one of our most dangerous inmates."

"What? No. This is my friend—" I protest.

"Maybe she was," Greg says, "But she's not anyone's friend now. Even the fae have disowned her."

"Don't believe him, BJ," Shauna pleads. She leans closer to the bars but is careful not to touch them. "They've confused me with someone else. Or maybe it's simply the age-old prejudice against the fae rearing its head once more. I'm not a trickster or liar. I'm just an itty bitty little pixie trying to survive in a dangerous world."

I want to believe her. I want to bend the bars of her cage and set her free. Unfortunately, my bullshit detector is going off.

"Why is she so dangerous?" I ask Greg.

"She was in the middle of fae and vamp wars. The vampires got the bright idea to start turning the fae prisoners they kidnapped."

"Wait," Alaric interrupts. "That's illegal. The vampires themselves made the rule against turning other supernaturals."

"Yeah," Greg shrugs. "Guess that biker group went renegade. And now we got all these new made vamps that are so bloodthirsty they'd suck the whole world dry if given half a chance." Leaning closer to us and lowering his voice, he adds, "Val and Marguerite wanted us to put them all down. But you guys only gave orders to lock 'em up. Sooo..." He holds his hands out in a 'what can you do' gesture.

Shauna suddenly slams against the bars. Her skin sizzles with the contact, but she does it again. And then again. "You can't put me down like a damn dog. And you can't keep starving me either! Give me blood, you bastards. And not that cold congealed stuff either. I need fresh meat." There's a desperation in her voice. I turn to meet her burning eyes as she peers out between the bars. She smiles at me and now I can see the long fangs.

"I want a taste of that god blood, BJ," Shauna says, licking her lips, still full and pouty as ever. I always used to tell her if pageant circuit hadn't gone down along with everything else, she would've been collecting crowns like nobody's business. In response she said that she'd hate to embarrass me that way.

Shauna was a shit talker. But a funny one. She always said stuff like that in a way that made it clear she was joking.

But now, she sounds like she's dead serious as she adds, "Fresh blood."

"Enough." A First Brood whacks a nightstick against the bars and Shauna falls back, sucking her knuckles.

Her eyes flick to Alaric, brightening.

"Who's this? I wouldn't mind having a bite of him too…"

I step in front of him, finally finding my voice. "This is my man, Shauna. Go find one of your own!"

"Oh," she smiles. "But I already did."

She gestures to someone behind her, urging them forward with a crooked finger. Alaric's breath catches in his throat as a second figure steps into the light. My mouth falls open as Trevor gives us both an enigmatic smile.

"Hello, BJ. Hello, brother," he says. "Welcome to hell."

THE END

Continue the series with the next book **Catch & Conquer, Mythverse Book 6**!

Want to know about all the latest releases? Sign up for our Newsletter at MarleyLynn.com! When you sign up you'll receive **FREE SHORT STORIES**—all set in the Mythverse!

CATCH & CONQUER SNEAK PEEK

Chapter 1

"I am going to tear open your throat and drink you dry," the vampire hisses, pulling at the chains that confine him to the table, his eyes roaming over my neck.

I sigh. So, it's gonna be one of those intakes. "Sir, do you have any family that we can notify about your incarceration?"

"Then I'll use your corpse as a shield when I claw my way out of here," he snarls, his fangs elongating just at the thought.

Okay, as a rule baby vamps are blood-soaked hangry jerkwads, but this one is being particularly dickish. He was found in an abandoned house surrounded by his kills. He'd been feeding on humans in the area and had taken out nearly an entire town.

It took two dozen harpies to bring him down. Harpies act as the police force and guards, hunting down all the supernatural baddies and bringing them here to Underworld Reformatory. But these weren't just any harpies—they were

First Brood; i.e., the best, the brightest, and the direct descendants of a newly minted goddess. Once the First Brood had this vamp chained, all they could get from him was his name. I glance down at the papers in front of me.

"Mr...eh...Kit." Apparently all they got was his *first* name. "You are accused of murdering over a hundred humans. Usually I have a partner here who works on a reformation strategy, a way to re-enter human society after you've been properly trained on how to behave in our world. But my partner didn't show up to work today, and I'm not known for being a pushover. I have to be honest. I'm really not seeing a way out of here for you."

The vampire isn't paying attention. By the way he's licking his lips I guess he's too busy fantasizing about how yummy my blood would be. I make a note on his file. He needs to get into detox, quick.

Most vampires are born, not made. That's because made vamps seem to have a bottomless hunger for blood. It's better to keep these baby vamps underfed when they're first turned. The more blood they drink in that first year the more dependent they become on it later in life.

Even worse, he was feeding when the harpies found him, which means that right now he probably feels like he just drained two semi-trucks worth of caffeine. I'd almost feel sorry for the guy, if it weren't for the way he's straining against his chains, desperate to kill me.

I close my folder and stand. He can't even manage speech right now—at least not anything worth hearing. Maybe after he has a few weeks without a fix, I can try again. Next time with my calm, sweet, "good cop," partner by my side, things could go a lot smoother. It will be a rough few weeks for Kit while he's straightening out, but it's the only way I see forward.

"I have a sister," he tells me, suddenly lucid, his fangs

receding slightly as he gains some control. I'm so surprised I forget that he's not just making an announcement; he's answering my question about if he had any family we could inform of his imprisonment.

I sit back down, snapping my folder open, ready to take notes. I nod at him, encouraging what seems to be his first rational train of thought since he was brought in.

"She's fae," he says. "But I turned her." His face twists for a second, as if he hates what he's saying.

"You turned your own sister?"

"I had to!" he yells, straining against the chains again. "She was dying! The other fae came after her when—"

"Wait," I stop him. "Is her name Shauna?" Fae/vamp hybrids searching for their siblings aren't exactly a common occurrence.

"How did you know that?" he asks, surprise making him look almost human for the half second it takes him to figure out that the only way I could know that would be if I already had his sister in lockup.

"I want my sister," Kit says, looking around wildly like she might just apparate into the intake room simply because he wishes it.

"I don't think that's going to be possible just now…"

I play for some time. I'm certainly not bringing Shauna to him. She's a pixie/vamp hybrid that I met IRL before she ended up in here. She'd seemed okay back then. Here at Underworld Reformatory we all secretly refer to Shauna as the *mosquito*. It's not just because she's a tiny bloodsucker. She's annoying as hell and screeched for three days when we first brought her in, the tiny whine of her voice filling everyone's ears.

"I. Want. My. Sister." Kit bites each word off, his fangs elongating again when I don't immediately cave to his wishes.

I push away from the table, bringing my file folder with me, and putting a hand to my hip where I keep my handy dandy ray gun.

Kit is now banging his hands on the table and yelling each word, shaking his chains for emphasis. "I. Want. My. Sister."

As I back out of the room he stands, and with a mighty lunge, rips the chains from the table. It upends, and now there's nothing between us but stale air. He charges with a hiss.

I sling my gun forward and shoot. A beam of light hits Kit square on the chest and he freezes with a cry of pain. He's supposed to slump to the ground, immobile. But instead he simply falls to one knee, glaring at me the whole time. With willpower that can only be born of a powerful bloodlust, he pushes himself back to his feet and lurches forward.

Fern, the witch who made this gun, was worried that a panicked guard might shoot a prisoner more than once. "The point of this stun gun is to preserve life on both sides," she had said, and my tender-hearted intake partner, Cassie, agreed. So Fern put a magical fail-safe on the weapon. You can shoot the gun as much as you want, but after the first shot, it will have no effect on the same person. Not until twenty-four hours pass; that way guards don't abuse their power…or the prisoners.

This is what happens when the people in charge are afraid of being seen as the bad guys. We get guns that only work once a day.

We're locking up all the dangerous paranormals. But we pretend it's temporary. We don't even call this a prison. It's a reformatory. Every prisoner gets a personalized plan to help them get out and rejoin society.

It's a joke. There is no world in which Kit and others like him won't be a menace.

Kit lunges desperately forward; my back is to the door. I

shoot again, but as I already knew it would—the shot has no effect on him. His hands close around my shoulders, squeezing hard enough to leave bruises as he brings my neck to his hungry fangs.

I manage to slip Mr. Freeze (yeah, I named my stun gun. It's stupid and dorky and no one knows about it except me, because it would totally mess with the badass persona image I try to project) back into his holster and then I shift.

In the blink of an eye, I shrink to the size of a small housecat. Though thankfully not one that's been declawed. Curling up one of my kitty paws, I swipe a claw across Kit's face before falling to the ground.

The vampire strength may have made him physically strong and fast, but his bloodlust has made him stupid. He blinks down at me, confused, as I scoot between his feet.

The door opens just in time and harpies enter the intake room. When the First Brood brought him in, he killed three of them, which their mother was *not* happy about. Technically, the three gods who serve as the Triumvirate aren't supposed to interfere with what we do here, but I wouldn't be surprised if Zahara (Mama harpy and one of the Triumvirate gods) made a sudden amendment to the rules and decided to deal with this baby vamp herself.

Even if she doesn't, he's going to have a hard time of it here in Underworld Reformatory; all of the guards are First Brood—Zahara's children. Which means that the harpies he took out were their siblings, and harpies aren't exactly the most forgiving of the supernatural species.

The First Brood wastes no time putting Kit back in chains, and I'm kind of glad Cassie isn't here to see it. Her sweet little heart would break at the sound of him calling for his sister. Even if he's a psycho and his sister's a total bitch.

I waste no time getting out the door and into the hallway where I shift back into human form.

Like my clothes, Mr. Freeze is magic so he shifts with me. I can't operate him with my little kitty paws, but I can still keep him close so long as he's holstered. Normally just having a hand on Mr. Freeze is enough to calm me. To make me feel safe.

But not today. Mr. Freeze has let me down.

Instead of staying on the job and helping the harpies with a crazed baby vamp, I walk away as fast as my legs will take me. With every step I fall apart a little more. My breathing grows uneven and my limbs start to shake.

By the time I get into the bathroom, I'm gasping for breath.

Grasping the edge of the sink, I stare into the mirror. "Get it together, Mavis," I tell myself. My voice trembles and I close my eyes, not wanting to see myself anymore. Hating how weak I've become.

I reach down the front of my shirt and pull out one of the pills I keep hidden inside of my bra. Like, Mr. Freeze, it's magic. Unlike him, it hasn't yet let me down. I swallow with a handful of water from the sink. A moment later, it's like someone put steel in my spine. I'm standing straight and tall and am ready for anything.

Buy now to continue reading **Catch & Conquer, Mythverse Book 6**!

Chapter 1

Cleaning up after a vampire rave sucks.

Pun intended.

My first one, I came armed with a whole truckload of hydrogen peroxide, expecting blood stains everywhere. In my mind, they covered the walls and floors and ceilings. I expected something like what a plasma donation center would look like if it was run by someone hopped up on way too much Mountain Dew.

It turns out, though, that vampires are not messy eaters. You might even say they don't like to waste a single drop of their meal. It's sacred to them the way Ho-Ho's were to my seventh-grade math teacher.

So yeah, it's not the prospect of scrubbing away blood stains that's getting me down as I drive through the warehouse district searching each building for the 6669 the vamps paint on the wall of their chosen party spot. The number's some sort of vampire humor, I think. Or maybe not. They're hard to read and I'm not interested in getting close enough to find out anything about them beyond that they pay in cash.

"Where is this stupid place?" I ask aloud, even though there's no one else in the van with me. Although...my van is kind of sentient. Like a cross between Christine and Herbie, it's both terrifying and adorable.

Vanna was stolen ages ago. Back when she...er, *it*, was just a normal Grand Caravan with stained seats and a dented back fender from some tailgating asshole. I figured that was the last I'd see of it, but a few months back I opened my door and there was Vanna (yes, I named her and yes I hate myself for it). The same...but also totally different.

I would've sent her straight back to the impound lot where she was found if it wasn't for the fact that I was desperate for transportation. The transmission had just died on my previous van and without wheels I had no job. So I used Vanna, figuring I could just pretend she was normal. Just another vehicle.

That didn't last long.

In response to my question, Vanna takes over steering, which is always annoying. But I forgive her as she parks us in front of a building, the 6669 on the wall straight ahead.

From the outside the warehouse looks totally unremarkable. Just another big boxy building. I can't hold back a big sigh as I grasp the handles on the giant sliding door. Putting all my weight into it, I pull the door hard. With a groan it gives way, gliding open and allowing a bright shaft of sunlight to cut through the dark interior.

"Aw fuck," I say as a giant water tank fills my vision. I'm not talking about some little pet store thing; this is Sea World size. I have no idea how I'm gonna drain this thing and scrub it spotless. That's the job, though. I'm supposed to leave only the dust motes and a sparkling clean tank behind when I'm done.

This alone would be a monumental task, but as I walk into the warehouse and closer to the tank and the moving shadows within, I know it's gonna get worse.

And it does.

Sharks. Big ones, too. They glide through the water with silent menace.

Those asshole vamps decided to have an underwater rave and feed on fucking sharks.

I thought the lions were the worst. Before that, I thought the pigs were the worst.

Clearly, I was wrong all those times. Because really, vampires are the worst. Always and forever—they are The. Worst.

I take a minute to swear viciously and creatively, cursing not just vampires but all the paranormal creatures that decided to come out of hiding a decade ago and totally screw up everything. Sometimes I hear people say that it's better to know than to live in ignorance. I disagree. The time when I believed that werewolves, harpies, and faeries were all just stories was a great time. An easier, simpler one too.

I was only in my early twenties when everything changed. My dad's cleaning business was struggling and I'd just graduated with a degree in English that I was quickly realizing was pretty much useless in the real world. Then we had a little apocalypse. Cities disappeared beneath the sea. Crops failed. And all the supes came out to play. Suddenly college degrees didn't mean much. Survival was our entire focus.

I got married to my boyfriend, 'cause it felt like we might all die and I guess I wanted to wear a white dress first? I don't know. It wasn't the greatest decision. I also went into business with Dad. But we revamped it. Pun intended.

Harper Cleaning became Down & Dirty: Supernatural Cleaning Services. Dad said we were kinda like the clean-up crew for the Ghostbusters. "Think about it," he'd say. "Someone had to mop up that marshmallow mess, and I bet they got paid good money. Hazard pay, right?"

He was right. The business thrived. My marriage failed. But overall, life was good.

Until my parents disappeared along with a few hundred thousand other folks.

But that's another story.

Right now, I gotta figure out how to get these sharks outta this tank.

Luckily, we're in the Newark Port district. I understand now why they chose this location. But still, the Bay is a good ten minutes away. Can a shark survive that long out of water?

Pulling out my phone, I start to Google.

Some people might think I'm just a cleaning lady, but in truth, this job requires way more than just a mop and broom.

Yesterday I was choking on feathers cleaning out a frat house that had been full of chicken shifter strippers. Today I'm wrestling sharks. Tomorrow I might be scrubbing harpy droppings off some vocal Humans First protester's roof and lawn.

Down & Dirty is more than just a job. It's a lifestyle.

R ead the whole 7 book series today!

ABOUT THE AUTHORS

DEMITRIA LUNETTA is the author of the YA books THE FADE, BAD BLOOD, and the sci-fi duology, IN THE AFTER and IN THE END. She is also an editor and contributing author for the YA anthology, AMONG THE SHADOWS: 13 STORIES OF DARKNESS & LIGHT. Find her at www.demitrialunetta.com for news on upcoming projects and releases. Or join the newsletter list for DEMITRIA LUNETTA

KATE KARYUS QUINN is an avid reader and menthol chapstick addict with a BFA in theater and an MFA in film and television production. She lives in Buffalo, New York with her husband, three children, and one enormous dog. She has three young adult novels published with HarperTeen: ANOTHER LITTLE PIECE, (DON'T YOU) FORGET ABOUT ME, AND DOWN WITH THE SHINE. She also recently released her first adult novel, THE SHOW MUST GO ON, a romantic comedy. Find out more at www.katekaryusquinn.com and make sure you're receiving newsletters from KATE KARYUS QUINN

MARLEY LYNN is a lost child of the gods, who waits on the shores of Lake Erie for her parents to bring her home. In the meantime, she contents herself with reading, writing, and gardening. Find out more at www.MarleyLynn.com or sign up for MARLEY LYNN'S newsletter.

ACKNOWLEDGMENTS

Thank you to Marin McGinnis for taking care of our copy edits!

And, of course, a big thank you to our families for putting up with us crazy writers.